1

88 ways to die

88 Ways to Die

ISBN: 978-0-6151-5115-1

Prelude

The electronics section of the department store was graced by over a dozen television sets ranging from thirteen to fifty inches. Over half of the sets were tuned to a mid day newscast. A brown-haired semi-gorgeous woman with a bright red lipstick enhanced mouth was the sole anchor.

"Police today are searching for the boy friend of a slain Chicago woman in connection with her bludgeoning death. Donna Beck, twenty-seven, was found slain in her home this morning when co-workers became worried when she didn't report to work."

A still photograph of a smiling innocent looking black woman flashed briefly across the screen.

"Miss Beck was an employee of the highly regarded IVS brokerage firm here in Chicago."

A blonde goddess dancing on the edge of tears appeared on camera. Superimposed on the bottom of the screen briefly were the words; FRANCINE DARDEN, CO-WORKER

"It was so unlike her not to report to work. You know, without calling first. So we were really worried by lunchtime. I don't know who would've wanted to kill her. She was so sweet. She didn't have an enemy in the world."

There was a cut back to the anchor.

"Neighbors reported a loud argument between Beck and her boy friend shortly before the murder occurred. Police wouldn't release the name of the boy friend. And they wouldn't say if he's considered a suspect at this point. Coming up after a break, more hard times for the White Soxs and Cubs."

Chapter 1

It was a good time to be in Chicago in 1988. The ice, slush, snow, and vicious blowing winds of winter had passed. In the interim between a steamy and hot summer, pleasant temperatures and bright, breezy days of spring filled the air.

Ellis Mason was seated on the driver's side of a black Volvo parked near the middle of a block on a street of old brownstone buildings with basement apartments and one or two stories above them.

Ellis was a medium brown-skinned man in his early thirties. He was just under six feet tall on a slender frame. His deep-set eyes and wide flared nose gave him a rugged appearance.

He was busy doing his job as a private investigator. He had been hired by ex-con Armad Drew to tail his girl friend, Donna Beck. Armad was worried about Donna possibly dating a man she had been involved with during his stay in prison. Ellis had been wary of taking the case. He wasn't sure how Armad would react if he received news he didn't like.

Fifteen minutes passed before a petite, cute brown-skinned black woman just above five feet tall emerged from a second floor apartment. She was dressed in a tight fitting bright red mini dress. She moved down the walk with a stride that said she knew she looked great, and would have no trouble exciting the man she planned to spend the evening with. She got into a light green compact car and drove straight up the block.

After pausing for several seconds, Ellis started his car and trailed Donna's. He quickly recognized the route she was taking. He knew she would stop at a one-story house covered by light blue aluminum siding.

Ellis parked behind Donna's car five doors down from the light blue house. He reached over and snapped the glove compartment open. From it he took a camera with a long lense attachment. Ellis aimed the camera outside the car window in time to snap several rapid-fire photos of Donna moving up the walk, ringing the doorbell and waiting for her lover to answer.

A lightskinned man with slicked down hair appeared in the doorway and embraced Donna and peppered her with kisses.

Ellis stayed parked for nearly a half-hour before deciding they were in for the night and no more photo opportunities were possible. He had enough material to justify his fee and provide evidence of an affair.

Ellis went home to his one story brick house located in the Chicago neighborhood of South Shore. In the living room, he removed his shirt and tossed it on the sofa. He left the room and returned with a can of beer. Ellis picked up the remote and clicked on the TV. He dialed around the channels, finding nothing interesting. His second time through he landed on a PBS talk show.

The host was a typical serious-expressioned PBS guy wearing a print sweater over a white shirt. He was interviewing candidates for a congressional district. The incumbent, Walter Ryan, and his challenger, James Cody. Ryan was a stocky guy in his mid forties with unruly dark red hair, narrow gray eyes, and a nose that looked like it had been broken more than once. Cody had a square-jawed farm boy look about him. His dark hair had a receding line that angled to the right toward a part.

The host said: "Now Mr. Cody, the Republican party has had a hard time in this part of the state, so what makes you think you can defeat an entrenched incumbent like Congressman Ryan?"

"I think we're coming into a new era of politics in this country. As we saw in the 84 presidential year, many Republicans rode the wave of Reagan popularity into office. I expect the same thing will occur with Mr. Bush. Plus the old days of overspending Democrats are over. People want big government out of their lives. The private sector has to be set free in order to stimulate the economy and bring prosperity to this country."

"Congressman, how do you respond?"

Ryan smiled dryly. "Let me say this. The Democratic Party has always delivered for the people of this city and county. And yes. We do need to stimulate the private sector. But I firmly believe the government still has a valuable role to play in its citizen's lives."

"Now uh. Since the district has been redrawn, it now encompasses a diverse economic and racial make up. From the affluent lakeshore and a portion of the northern suburbs to black and Hispanic wards. How do you appeal to such a varied group of voters?"

"There's only one way you can do it," Ryan said. "You do your best to make people's lives-"

Ellis had seen enough. He clicked off the set.

The following morning, Donna Beck lounged in her bed reviewing in her mind how thoroughly glorious her lovemaking session with her lover, Randy, had been the previous evening. The man knew how to make her tingle. From every orifice, from the top of her head all the way down to her toes.

She recalled a conversation they had.

"Are you doing the right thing, baby?" Randy had asked.

"What's right? All I know is I've been kicked in the ass all my life. Now it's time for me to kick some ass."

Chapter 2

Cody was in a very good mood as he tooled toward the Loop in his Lincoln. At the age of forty-two he felt like he was on the verge of finally accomplishing something on his own. His life had been relatively easy compared to most. He grew up in the Illinois sate capital of Springfield.

His father was a partner in a prestigious law firm that had been founded by his grandfather. It seemed pre-destined that he also would become a lawyer. He was never prodded toward a career in law but the ambience and allure was always hanging in the air he breathed. When he was old enough he attended some of his father's trials. Although fascinated by his father's court persona, it was the prosecutor's approach to law that intrigued him. Only his family was surprised that after he completed law school and passed the bar, he wanted to use his talents working for the state. Reluctantly, his father pulled enough strings to get him on the staff of the State's Attorney in Chicago. He steadily climbed the ladder to the point where he was handling a high percentage of high profile cases that came through the office. His success rate brought him to the attention of down state Republican bigwigs. They convinced him that he could be a viable congressional candidate. Against his father's advice, Cody jumped in with both feet. Now, after the television appearance, he was flying high and feeling good about his chances.

Cody left his car in a downtown parking garage. Although his advisors were a little worried, he enjoyed driving in alone, leaving his car and walking to his campaign headquarters.

At a street corner waiting for the light to change, Cody stood next to a plump woman in her forties.

"You are him. You're James Cody, aren't you?"

"Guilty as charged."

"I've been listening to you. I like it. I support you. I may want to work for you."

"We need all the volunteers we can get." Cody reached inside his suit coat pocket and removed a business card. "If you really want to work for us, call the number and ask for Maggie."

"Oh I will. I will."

Cody turned on the avenue and started toward State Street. The driver of a parked car poked his head out of the window.

"Hey Cody. Saw you on TV last night. "Give 'em hell!"

Cody smiled and waved at the driver. "I will."

The campaign headquarters had once been a fashionable boutique. Red printed letters on a yellow background simply stated its purpose, It said:

CODY CAMPAIGN HEADQUARTERS

Inside, several desks were jammed into the front room. Most of the workers manning the phones and performing other duties were women, with a smattering of college aged men thrown into the mix.

Cody strode into the headquarters. He waved, greeted, and shook hands with workers on his march to his private office.

Expensive but bare bones furnishings and equipment dominated Cody's inner office. A thin partitioned wall divided the room into a pair of offices. A smaller one for his office manager, and another, which contained an oak desk and a long oblong clear plastic conference table.

Cody stepped in and veered toward the office of Maggie Bowen, an energetic and perky woman in her mid fifties. She was busy banging on a computer and engaging in a phone conversation. Cody waited until she was off the phone.

"Good morning gorgeous."

"Hello Mr. TV star."

"How are things popping so far today?"

"Quite well, thank you. We've had some positive calls about the show last night. Some potential contributors."

"That's always nice to hear."

"I've got the ladies doing as little informal poll. I'd be surprised if we don't see a boost in name recognition and support. I have a feeling things will be looking up."

"Amen to that. Knock on wood."

Ryan skipped down the stairs of his suburban home and went to the telephone table just off the staircase. He dialed a number.

"Hello."

"Hello there. It's me, doll. Have you got many calls, you know, about the show last night?"

"Not really. But the one's we've gotten have been positive."

"Just like it should be, huh? We'll be all right. Democrats rule. Am I right?"

"You're right."

Ellis sat in his car in the small parking lot next to his business. The structure was located on a block of businesses on the West Side. It was a small place on a corner lot. The sign out front said: MASON DETECTIVE AGENCY

At times, Ellis gazed at his business and was amazed that it had lasted four years. It had been a long haul getting there. He had gone to college two years with the idea of becoming an accountant. He lost interest. Plus scraping up college money was a problem for him and his parents. He bounced around from job to job until he landed with a security company. Ellis was contemplating leaving for a higher paying position when the company decided to expand the business into divorce work, document serving, and locating missing persons. A boost in pay, training, and more interesting work made him stick around.

Ellis was bitten by the bug of wanting to start his own security firm. He took business and criminal justice classes, and looked into small business loans. The early stages of the operation cost him income, which didn't bother him. But it also cost him his marriage, something that upset him for several months until he came to the realization that there was nothing he could do to rectify the situation.

Inside the agency, there was wood grain paneling along the walls in the reception area. A narrow hall led to an equipment and storage area, and straight ahead to Ellis' office.

At the desk out front was Maybeline Connors, a round-faced medium-brownskinned woman nearing thirty.

Ellis entered the office.

"Well hello," Maybeline said. "For once you're right on time."

"That's why I'm the boss. So I can come in a little late. Where's your brother?"

"He went around the corner to get some coffee and doughnuts. We didn't have time to eat anything for breakfast."

"Have you heard from our Muslim buddy?"

"No."

"Damn. If we don't hear from him by this time tomorrow, we'll just have to tell him to get somebody else to handle the security for his event."

J.C Connors came through the door carrying a box of coffee cups and a bag of doughnuts.

"People, people, people. Hello people. The goodies have arrived."

J.C had his sister's round features. His hair was cut down close to his skull. His face seemed flat and nondescript until he smiled, and everything about him was illuminated. He was twenty-four.

The coffee and doughnuts were placed on the desk by J.C. He popped the lid of a container of coffee and drank from it.

"So what's on the slate for today?" Are you still stalking the babe for my man Armad?"

"No. That's pretty much wrapped. All I have to do is get him in and drop it on him. I just hope the brother will stay cool."

"I think he will."

"I hope he will."

Chapter 3

Brad Royce left the office building and stepped onto the sidewalk. He wore a tan Armani suit, pastel gold shirt, and a dark brown solid tie. In his late twenties, Royce had preppy All-American features topped with close-cropped light brown hair.

Royce approached the waiting cab, sliding into the back seat. The Arab driver mumbled something in his language when Royce requested the short ride into the Loop.

Four people were assembled in the office conference room. Cody was there along with his campaign manager, John Brooks, a world weary, gray haired man in his fifties. Also present was Marty Silver, a political consultant extraordinare. He was a balding guy with deep set eyes, and a salt and pepper beard and mustache.

The lone woman was Andrea Newsome. She was tall and slinky and had short-cropped black hair with bangs. She had arching eyebrows, narrow light green eyes, a thin straight nose, and small pouty lips. She was Silver's associate.

Royce stepped into the room. "Good morning everybody. Sorry if I'm a little late. I had to deal with a lost and confused cab driver."

Brooks stood and shook Royce's hand. "Hello Brad. Good to see you again. I know you recognize Mr. Cody. This is Mr. Silver and Ms Newsome, our political consultants."

Royce shook hands with Silver. He reached to take Andrea's hand by the fingertips but she turned it into a traditional handshake. She flashed a brief pleasant smile in his direction. It was enough to spark interest in her by Royce.

"Have a seat," Brooks said. "Let's begin. Go into a little detail about what we want from you. As you may know, our campaign is about ready to kick into high gear. The television appearance last night was the first big kick off. According to all the polls, James will not just be a token candidate. He has a legitimate chance of unseating Ryan. Which means things could get a little nasty."

"What we have to do, is be ready to fight fire with fire," Cody interjected.

"We want your agency to do a thorough investigation into Ryan's background. If you find anything that's not too kosher, go with it to the hilt. You know, I'm not too fond of operating in this manner, but it seems to be the way of the world. These days at least."

"I suppose you have to do what you have to do," Royce said. "It seems to me I do recall Ryan being under fire for awarding a contract to a company he used to work for before he was elected."

"Yes. But nothing ever came of it. The company seemed to have made a legit low bid. You won't have any qualms about delving in Ryan's personal life. You know, marital infidelity, psychiatric care."

"Not a all. It's all part of doing the right thing for the job."

Cody leaned forward in his chair and locked his fingers together in front of him. "I'm sure you understand that I don't wish to be linked directly to this uh, operation. You'll be making reports to Mr. Silver."

"Actually, you'll be coming to me," Andrea said.

"I'll have no problem with coming to you."

Royce's tone was suggestive. He wished he could have returned the words to his mouth before they became audible. He surmised that he would have very little chance of getting anywhere with Andrea.

The metal desk in Ellis' office was always cluttered with papers and other business related paraphernalia. There were two photographs encased in a frame folder. One was of his four year-old daughter, Keisha. The second was his current girl friend, Zoe, who some said favored his ex-wife, Carmen.

Black cushioned chairs were positioned around the desk. A few feet from the desk was a table on which a computer and fax machine rested.

Ellis was seated at his desk going over paper work when Armad Drew sauntered in.

Armad was a muscular, broad-shouldered stocky man in his late twenties. His mahogany complexion, shaved head, and killer eyes game him a hard-nosed appearance.

"Armad. My man. Come on in and sir down."

Armad moved over and sat in one of the chairs near the desk.

"So. What's the four one-one on my baby, Donna?"

Ellis searched through the clutter on his desk and secured a file folder. "The news ain't too good, man. But I guess you need to know."

Armad yanked the file containing surveillance photos and activity logs from Ellis' grasp. He opened the file, scanning quickly through the photos, and ignoring the log. He rose to his feet angrily.

"Goddamn that bitch. She played me like a sucker." Armad began to pace back and forth. "Bitch! I'll kill her ass. I'll kill her ass."

Ellis rose to his feet. "Come on, man. You can't do that. You don't wanna end up back in the joint, do you?"

"Shit naw. But I can't be played. I can't be played for no chump."

"Look, what you have to do is calmly sit down and talk to her. Find out if you can fix things up, or just move on. That's my advice. Does it sound cool to you?"

"Yeah. Yeah. You speaking right."

Armad turned to exit the office

A staff meeting was being held in the richly furnished conservatively decorated conference room at Royce Investigations. Royce was there along with a couple department heads and the company president, Josh Allison, a dapper man in his early sixties. He had been with Royce's father since he started the agency thirty years ago.

"We have a high priority case brought to us earlier by Mr. Royce. Nice work Mr. Royce. We've received a five thousand-dollar retainer from the client. Of course, we'll be doing a hundred percent background check on Congressman Walter Ryan. We'll send out a team to run down old friends and enemies from the past. Electronically, we'll check all the usual sources and contacts. For a week to ten days we'll have round the clock twenty-four hour surveillance on our subject. This will begin as soon as possible."

"I know my dad wouldn't like it, but I want to get in on the surveillance detail," Royce said.

"I won't tell if you don't."

The investigation of the life and times of Walter Ryan swung into operation. The search for political colleagues with axes to grind against him. The check for any type of disciplinary actions or complaints dating back to his high school days. Through computer link up the checking of credit status, financial dealings, the presence of his name on mailing lists of hate or porno operations.

Royce lived in a spacious bachelor type apartment on the Gold Coast. He had the room loaded down with electronic toys. A wide screen TV, VCR, CD player, video cameras, and his own personal set of electronic bugging devices.

On the walls in the room were collectible authentic vintage movie posters. There were posters from the films The Big Sleep, Maltese Falcon, and Chinatown.

Royce knew the realities of being a private investigator, but it was the hyped up glamorous myth that intrigued him. He hoped to one day be involved in a dangerous and exciting case.

Royce had just slipped on a pair of light gray pinstriped slacks. He moved to a closet with a sliding wooden door. From the closet he removed a medium pink dress shirt and a pink and gray striped tie.

The phone on a table near the bed sounded off. Royce slid over and lifted the receiver.

"Hello."

"Hey, it's me. Wallace."

"Yeah. How is it going so far?"

"Just routine stuff. He went from an appearance to lunch. And then back to his headquarters. He hasn't left since then. I have to ask you about doing me a little favor. My wife called and said she'll be late getting home from work. So I need to get off a little early to pick my kid up from school."

"Sure. I'll be there as quick as I can. Probably in about twenty minutes."

She glided down the street like a woman that had to be somewhere in a hurry. She was so stunningly beautiful, even dressed in a below the knee business suit, she turned a lot of heads. She had straight shoulder length honey blonde hair, big ocean blue eyes, and a bow-like mouth.

Francine Darden stopped at the Ryan campaign headquarters and disappeared inside.

Royce investigations had an operative on the opposite side of the street from Ryan's headquarters. When he saw Francine go inside he ducked into a doorway. He pulled out a walkie-talkie and spoke into it.

"Hey. I've got a little development. A hot blonde in light blue just went in. It could be something big, but maybe not."

"A hot blonde can't be all bad," Royce quipped.

Royce was in a company car parked a couple hundred feet down from the rear of Ryan's campaign headquarters. Forty minutes after he received the walkie talkie report Francine exited the headquarters carrying a briefcase. She paced about and checked the street as if waiting for a ride. A few minutes later a black limousine tooled onto the street and parked. It was then that Ryan emerged from inside. To most it would look like a boss and his co-worker heading out to a business appointment, but Royce was a bit more skeptical.

"I've got a blonde babe and Ryan in a limo together," Royce said into his walkie-talkie. "I think I better tag along."

Royce watched the limo head north. He waited a few moments and took off behind it. The limo hit Lake Shore Drive, stayed on a minute, and cut down a couple blocks before turning left and stopping in front of an upscale apartment building.

Royce pulled the car over and parked. He saw Francine leave the limo and stride toward the building entrance. The limo did something he didn't expect. Instead of driving away it moved along and swung into the resident's parking lot.

Royce wondered what the hell was going on.

Five minutes later he found out. Ryan came from the parking lot, now donning dark glasses and a fedora. He went inside the building.

It suddenly came clear to Royce. Dress your babe up in a nice business outfit. Drop her off at the door. Hang out a few minutes in the parking lot. And then come around and ask to see a pre-arranged accomplice. Pretty smart, Mr. Ryan. But not smart enough.

Royce waited a couple minutes before exiting his car and moving to the apartment building. In the vestibule there was doorman, a beefy guy in his thirties, who was in charge of buzzing up, and letting people inside.

"Good afternoon, sir. How can I help you?" the doorman asked.

"Uh. The thing is. I'm Dr. Rodgers. I'm embarrassed to say this. The young lady in blue that just came in. I've uh. Seen her at the hospital a time or two. And I. I saw her leaving just as I was. And I. I just had this impulse to follow her wherever she was going.
Hopefully home. She does live here, doesn't she?"

"What are you? A pervert. A stalker?"

"No, no, no. I'm not. I assure you," Royce said convincingly.

"I just want to know her name. I could find out from another source. But since I'm here."

The doorman seemed to shut down for several seconds. Finally, he said: "Her name is Francine Darden."

Donna Beck paced back and forth across the carpet on her living room floor with a phone receiver to her ear.

"I'm worried about this, Benny. I really am. I have the feeling people are watching me everywhere I go."

"Come on girl. You're being paranoid. We're cool. We're in control."

"I'm not so sure."

"Will you stop. You said you wanted to change your life. Are you going to wimp out on me?"

"No. No."

"Good girl. That's what I like to hear."

Chapter 4

Francine lay in her queen size bed covered by satin sheets. Her mind flashed back to the night before when she had sex with Ryan. It wasn't a grand experience for her. She almost never reached ultimate pleasure with him. Yet she felt she was getting what she wanted out of the relationship.

To be honest, her life in Chicago hadn't gone like she had envisioned when she left her small southern Illinois hometown beaming with high hopes. She faced a tough road trying to make her dream of becoming a high fashion model a reality. Mostly because her five-six and a quarter height was under the desired five-eight and above ideal. To keep her head above water she used her secretarial and management skills. As if on a pre-destined collision course, she found herself constantly crossing paths with local politicians. Then she began working for them. They gave her gifts and money, sometimes without her ever asking.

Now, here she was the mistress of an important comgressman-businessman, living in a swank apartment with a view of the lake. Not exactly her dream come true, but far from being a nightmare experience.

Michelle Grant moved through a workroom at Royce Investigations with a file folder clutched under her arm. She was a shapely black woman in her mid twenties. She had a cute, baby-faced look, carmel complexion, and sultry bedroom eyes. She had a braided corn row hairdo that stopped just above her shoulders.

Michelle rapped on the office door.

"Come in."

When she entered Royce's office he was viewing a videotape

highlighting the Bears 1985 Super Bowl victory.

"Are you watching that thing again?"

"I can't help myself. They were a damn great team. The best I've ever seen. I still can't believe we lost at home to Washington two years in a row."

"I don't know what Ditka was doing with Flutie in eighty-six. Maybe we'll get back to the top this year. I have a print out on Miss Darden's background check."

Michelle came over and placed the folder on the desktop.

"Give me the highlights."

Royce used the remote to click off the portable TV.

"Miss Darden is employed by the IVS brokerage firm. As an executive secretary. She uses Visa and MasterCard. She has charge accounts. Carson's and Marshall Field's. Lives in a pretty high rent North side apartment. And she's still making payments on a BMW."

"I'm getting the picture. Either she's the highest paid executive secretary in Chicago, or she's getting a little help from her friends."

"Are you thinking that Congressman Ryan could be her sugar daddy?"

"I would say that he's a prime candidate, so to speak."

Cody and Andrea sat side by side at the table in his campaign headquarters office. Cody was reading over a speech Andrea had written for him.

Andrea looked Cody straight in the face. "How do you like the speech? Does it hit home the points you want to make?"

"Pretty much. Yes, I like the way you slam Democrats for their tired ideas. And for being big government big spenders."

"I think it paves the way for your tax relief and incentives to businesses programs."

"Uh, there is something I'd like to bring up to you. With these minorities in my district, how do I appeal to them?"

"Well. Our studies show that they may have the lowest turn out of any ethnic groups. Especially blacks since, you know, the death of Washington. And they've become splintered. More importantly, they've usually been solid in the Democratic camp. But there is a group we may be able to appeal to. Yuppie types out to climb the corporate ladder. Business owners, and maybe ministers with self help programs."

"Wow. I'm impressed. You people are really thorough."

"We try to be."

Chapter 5

Donna Beck was again dressed in red. This time it was under dire circumstances. Red would be the last color she would ever wear in her life. Her body was covered in a red bathrobe. She was on the floor of the living room lying on her stomach, her legs in a modified spread eagle position, her arms outstretched. A splotch of drying blood covered the back of her head just to the left of center. Less than two feet away there rested a bloodstained metal cylinder-shaped lamp.

A co-worker on her lunch hour had discovered the body after Donna didn't show up for work, or call in to explain her absence. Now, a homicide crew had arrived on the scene. A photographer had just walked through the door.

Homicide detective Norris Leech paced about in a semi-circle. He was a thin man of medium height. He looked more like a schoolteacher than a cop.

An uniformed cop stepped inside. "Hey Norris. I've got a lady here that heard something."

"I'm on my way."

Leech stepped out onto the second floor porch area. A tired looking black woman in her fifties was present.

"This is Mrs. Jenkins," the uniformed officer said. "She heard something important last night."

"I'm detective Leech. Tell me what you heard, ma'am."

"It was a. A fight between that poor child and her so-called boy friend."

"Do you know the boy friend's name?"

"Yeah. Yeah. It's uh. Armad something. Uh, uh Drew. That's it."

"Are you sure it was Drew you heard?"

"Oh yeah. I've heard them argue before. I knowed the voice. I don't know why she stayed with him. One time he chased the poor child out the house in nothing but a pair of panties."

"Do you remember what time it was when you first heard the argument?"

"Oh. Let me see. I was watching Johnny Carson. So it wasn't after eleven-thirty. It was probably around eleven, but I wouldn't bet the rent money, you understand?"

Several hours later, Ellis was in his office preparing to leave for the day when the phone rang.

"Hello. Mason Detective Agency."

"Hey homie. This is Armad."

"Yeah. What's up, man?"

"I'm in big trouble, man. Five-O busted me on suspicion of murder."

"Did you do it?"

"No, man. I swear. You know how Five-O is. She's dead. I'm her man. So I must've done it. If they come up with any half-assed evidence they gonna charge me with murder."

Ellis was skeptical. "Come on man. They must have some reason to suspect you."

"Okay, I'm gonna tell you. I did like you said. I went to talk to her. But it turned into a fight. But she was alive when I left. I need you to represent me, man."

"You need a lawyer, don't you?"

"I'll get a shyster. But I may need you to prove somebody else had a reason to kill her."

"I don't know. This is outta my league. Divorce type work is one thing. But murder is something else."

"Hey look uh, my old man left me a little nest egg. I'll pay you double your usual rate. My sister can arrange it."

"I just don't know about this."

"At least come down and talk to me. I've got some more shit to put to you, but I can't talk about it on the phone."

"All right. I'll come. I'll be there."

On the drive to the police station, Ellis wondered what Armad's full story would be. He also wondered if an ex-con was doing a major con job on him.

Ellis was able to talk to the police into letting them use an interrogation room to meet in rather than a crowded cell. An uniformed cop led them into a room that contained only a wooden desk and a couple chairs.

Armad sat in one of the chairs. Ellis moved opposite him and leaned against the edge of the table.

"Let's get started with this thing," Ellis said. "Tell me what made you want to go see Donna."

"It was those pictures. Those damn pictures. They stuck in my head all the time I was at work. I got home, and I. I tried to hold out, but I had to go over there and see her."

"Were you drinking before you went over there?"

Armad hesitated. "Okay. Yeah. But I wasn't drunk I drove over okay. When I hit her with what I knew I just thought she was at least gonna pretend like she was sorry. But then she hit me with all that you don't own me shit. That's what really got me pissed. I admit it. I pimp slapped her a couple times. I picked up this lamp to hit her with it, but uh, I stopped myself. I took my ass out the house and went into the back yard. I started yelling at her foolish ass to come out and talk to me. She wouldn't do it, so I cut on outta there."

"What time was it when you left?"

Armad ran his hand across his bald head. "I don't. It's too fuzzy. I can't remember."

"You better try to. It could be important. Go back and start from when you left the house."

"Uh. Let me see. I think I cut the TV off right before I left. The sports had just gone off. So I guess it must've been just before ten-thirty."

"How long does it take to go from your place to her's?"

"About fifteen to twenty minutes."

"How long did the fight last?"

"That I really don't know. It was like one of those things where everything happened in slow motion."

"Could you guess?"

"It couldn't be more than fifteen minutes. I probably was outside trying to cool off, and trying to talk to Donna for another fifteen minutes."

"So you were gone before eleven-thirty. Where did you go right after you left Donna's place?"

"I went to a bar on the South side called Rap City. I drank even more. And I. I met a woman there. And we went back to her place."

"What's her name?"

"Name. Man. I didn't even know where I was when I woke up in the middle of the night. She was out real bad. I just got up and got out of there. I was walking down the street and saw a cab. I was lucky I had some money in my pocket. That's how I got home."

Ellis pulled the chair out and sat down. "So far you haven't given me much to hang my hat on believing you. If you didn't kill Donna, somebody else must've had a reason. What kind of person was she? Was she involved with anything that could've gotten her killed?"

"She was a cool babe," Armad said as he leaned back in his seat. "She had a nasty mouth when she got mad. She had a little devious streak in her. But that didn't bother me none."

"Was this devious stuff illegal?"

"Not that I know of. But uh. I remember her mentioning that she and a friend had something big cooking."

"Do you know what that big plan was?"

"No. She didn't want to say. So I didn't press it."

"What about her friend's name?"

"She's a hot little white babe. Francine Darden."

"Do you know where she lives?"

"No. But she and Donna worked together. At a brokerage place. IVS. So are you with me, my brother?"

Ellis placed his elbow on the tabletop. He ran his fingers across his forehead. "I'll tell you what. I'll work it for a couple days. If I find something. I'll stay on it. Is that cool with you?"

"I guess it'll have to be."

"Let's get back to when you were at Donna's house. Where was your car parked? In the front or back?"

"The back."

"Damn. It's a better chance somebody would've seen your car leave around eleven-thirty if it had been parked out front. But I'll still look into it."

"You don't have to, man. My lawyer has somebody that'll do that shit. I need you to get me sprung outta here."

"I'll give it my best shot."

Andrea stepped into the bedroom of her apartment with only a wet towel wrapped around her hair. Her thin, but not too skinny, body had no excess body fat, and was quite muscular, considering she seldom had time to go through a full work out regiment. She had tear drop shaped breasts topped by dark pink nipples. Her pubic hair consisted of a rectangular patch no more than an inch wide.

Andrea stood in front of the dresser mirror. She liked what she saw. A tailor made exercise and nutrition program kept her looking the way she wanted. A move to a closet with a mirrored sliding door gave her another chance to gaze upon her nude body.

From the closet she removed an expensive low cut black dress just this side of being sheer? Andrea carried the dress to the bed and gently laid it out flat.

It amused her that the amount she spent on the dress was more than her father earned in a month back in the central Indiana town where she grew up. In her early years she was always the fattest kid in her classes, making her the target of ridicule. Yet teachers were constantly praising her for her dedication and her ability to make great grades. Also thrown into the mix was her mother being an ardent feminist in a conservative town. Mrs. Newsome caught flack for her political stances and protest demonstrations, but she had been able to come away with concrete victories.

By the time she reached high school Andrea had lost sixty pounds and all traces of acne. She was suddenly a steamy babe. She delighted in getting attention from boys who used to make fun of her. She delighted in having sex with them and then cold heartedly dumping them. The thrill of the vengeance was tempered by the "bad girl" reputation she earned. Andrea changed her tactics by dating one boy at a time. She learned how to cajole, seduce, and mesmerize them into doing exactly what she wanted them to do.

In college she majored in Political Science. To the delight of her father, and dismay of her mother, she became a member of the Young Republicans. After college she easily found work as a speechwriter for local and state Republican candidates. Through contacts and reputation she gained work as a campaign manager for a congressional candidate that had no chance of winning. It was a feather in Andrea's cap that he made a much better showing than expected. Two years later she was offered a position with Silver's consulting firm. At the time Silver was on a major roll. Lately, his gold star had become a little tarnished. Andrea was confident things would rebound. If not, she could move on to something else.

Andrea had slipped the black dress on and added a pair of black high heels. She scooped her purse off the dresser top and exited the room with a confident stride.

Rap City was called Rap City because all the music they played was either rap or hip-hop. Consequently the crowd they drew was young, black and hip, with a sprinkling of
Hispanics and whites, plus a few older people who put up with the music to take advantage of the low cost drinks.
To fit in a little more, Ellis came dressed in a baseball cap and a navy blue and orange Bears starter jacket. He weaved his way through the tables to the bar and sat on a stool.

The bartender was a tall skinny black man with a missing front tooth and thinning combed back hair. He moved to Ellis and said:

"My man. What can I get you?"

"I'll have a beer."

The bartender went to a tap and filled a mug with beer. He placed it before Ellis.

"Thanks, brother. Can I ask you something? Do you know Armad Drew?"

"Who's asking and why? Are you a cop?"

"No." He drank from his beer. "I'm a private investigator."

"Aw man. You another Shaft, huh."

"Or Sam Spade. What I'm doing is trying to help Armad out of a jam. Do you remember him being here last night?"

"Yeah. He was here."

"Do you remember what time he got here?"

"Sorry. I was pretty busy. I couldn't say."

"What about when he left?"

"I can't say for sure. Just that it was awhile before we closed at two."

"Did he leave with someone?"

"Yeah. He cut out with a fly little brown babe."

"Do you know her name?"

"Naw. She wasn't no regular."

"Do you remember what she looks like?"

"Yeah. I think so."

Ellis gulped down more of his beer. He removed a card and several bills from his wallet. He put a couple bills on the bar top.

"This is for the beer." He handed a ten spot and a business card to the bartender. "If she comes in here again give me a call at one of these numbers. Try to get her name if you can. Okay?"

"Yeah. Cool."

Adrea slinked into the classy upscale River North restaurant. She scanned the room until she spotted the man she sought. She moved in his direction at a deliberate pace.

The man Andrea moved toward sat alone at a table. He had a deep, even tan that contrasted well with his full head of prematurely white hair. In his early fifties, he had a twinkle in his eyes, and handsome continental features. He wore a thousand dollar black silk suit over a collarless white shirt. His tie clamp and cuff links were diamond studded.

Andrea reached the table. The man stood and took her right hand gently, kissing it.

Ryan and Francine were under the covers together in her bedroom. They had just finished making love.

"How are things coming with the campaign?" Francine asked.

"Fairly well. This Cody guy may be a tougher opponent than I expected."

"You're not really worried about losing, are you? This county is a Democratic domain. This Cody guy is just a yuppie pretender."

Outside, on Francine's street, a pair of operatives from Royce Investigations were parked on the block in a dark blue Ford. On the driver's side was a beefy man with a thick mustache. Next to him was a young yuppie type guy. The beefy guy was munching on onion rings and gulping down a Coke.

"You know, it's a cruel world," the beefy guy said. "Here I am,a handsome hefty man wasting my night away sitting out here with you. And there is Ryan, another handsome hefty man, up in an apartment doing humpty dumpty type stuff with a young babe almost young enough to be his daughter."

"Don't take it so hard. You still have me to hang out with."

"Like I said. It's a cruel world."

"I hear Royce wants to switch tactics come tomorrow. They're worried Ryan may catch on to the fact that he's being followed. They want to put us on the babe. Let her lead us to him. See where she banks and spends money. See who her friends are in case we need to talk to them."

The beefy guy took a long swig from the Coke. "That's us. Work, work, work. For my boy Ryan, it's screw, screw, screw. Screw us the voters. Screw the little Darden babe."

Ryan had gotten into his shirt and pants. He was slipping on his socks. Still naked, Francine was stretched out in the bed in her stomach. Ryan eyed the contours of her perfect body and couldn't resist running his fingers down the small of her back to her buns.

"You're so goddamned beautiful, it's unbelievable. I hate to have to leave you."

"Don't worry. You'll be seeing me again soon."

"Well. Oh. The thing is. Maybe I won't be able to see you as much as I have been."

Francine rose to her knees. "Why the hell not? Are you tired of me?"

"Come on, doll. You know that's not true. I just uh. I have to be careful. The campaign is going full swing now. I'm going to be under a lot of scrutiny. I'm not trying to ease you out of my life."

"That's what it sounds like to me."

Francine stepped out of bed and stormed across the room. Ryan raced to catch up to her.

"Come on now. You know I care about you. Look how I take care of you. How I put things in your name. Look. I. I promise to find a way to see you as much as possible. All right? Okay?"

Francine whirled about with a big smile on her face. She threw herself into Ryan's arms.

"You're just so goddamn good to me."

"I already have an investigator that I use," the hook-nosed man in a bad, ill fitting suit said. He was Henry Snell, attorney at law. "But Armad insisted he wanted to use you, which is okay with me."

Ellis sat across from Snell near his beat up desk. "I'm only committed to a couple days."

"That may be a smart move on your part. I don't know how much investigating is needed."

"Are you saying you think Armad is guilty?"

"Well you can't rule it out. Look at his record. He did time for assault. Three years for manslaughter."

"Have you got a copy of the police report?"

"Yeah. Right here somewhere."

Snell searched through the clutter on his desk and came up with a file folder.

"I'll tell you. It's not too encouraging. Miss Beck was killed with a blunt instrument. Namely a lamp found near the body. And guess who's prints were on the lamp."

"He told me he picked up the lamp during an argument, but didn't carry through and use it."

"At least that's what he said. Let's see, uh, they got one neighbor that heard them arguing. And another that saw and heard Armad's car speeding away."

"Did the neighbor say what time the car left?"

"No. But there's a time of death estimate. From 11:45 to 12:45."

"Armad said he was gone from the house by eleven-thirty. He also puts himself at a bar called Rap City. It might give him an alibi for the time of death."

"Cross your fingers and knock on wood," Snell said sarcastically.

"I can tell you're going to mount a great defense if the case gets to court," Ellis countered.

"I'll do my job when the time comes. Even though I'm overloaded here. I just ain't got nothing to work with. Except the word of an ex-con."

"He said he was with a woman he met at the bar."

"Why didn't you say that before? Hell, if you find the woman I might use you as my investigator instead of this other guy."

"That gives me something to really shoot for."

Andrea slid the videotape into place. The twenty-one inch TV had been moved to the center of the lavish office. Cody sat in a chair near the desk.

"This is a rough cut without the music and graphics."

Andrea hit the ON switch. The setting of the commercial was a rich looking tree dotted park. From a medium long shot Cody strode confidently toward the camera. A God-like male voice over narrator said:

"Ronald Reagan started the revolution that put this country back on track. Now it's time to bring the revolution to Cook County. Because, let's face it, what has the Democratic party done for you lately?"

Quick cut still photographs were inserted. A shot of arguing, racially divided Chicago city council members, deserted factories that had been closed, policemen leading handcuffed suspects, mostly young black men, to a paddy wagon.

A tighter shot of Cody, looking presidential in a dark suit.

"James Cody. A new man with the right kind of old ideas," pronounced the narrator.

Andrea stopped the tape. "How do you like it?"

"Fantastic. I love it. You people really know what you're doing."

Ellis' Volvo was parked a couple buildings down from Francine's. Maybeline had been able to put together a decent file on Francine, including her address.

The sun was well on its way down when Ellis watched Francine exit her building dressed in a hot pink way above the knee mini dress. She moved toward the parking lot. Several seconds later her burgundy BMW pulled into traffic. Ellis waited a few moments before trailing after her. He never paid any special attention to the car behind his as it pulled away a couple seconds later.

Ellis followed Francine West across State Street to a black neighborhood.

He wondered where she was going. To buy drugs? Hang at a dance club? Or to date some homeboy on the side?

Ryan was to be a guest speaker at a black church's community center. The theme for the evening was community redevelopment, how it could be achieved, and what were the costs?

Had she not been dressed provocatively, Francine still would've attracted attention in the crowd of about two hundred because she was the only white woman present. As she stalked in primed to the max, heads turned, men's mouths popped open, and women's eyes rolled.

Ryan didn't witness the entrance due to him standing with his back turned as he mingled with the panel of experts assembled near the front of the meeting hall.

Francine moved halfway to Ryan and stared in his direction. Just when he sensed her presence and cut his eye in her direction, Francine smiled, waved, and reversed herself. It was as if she could feel Ryan's eyes boring into the back of her neck. He wouldn't be able to help himself. This wasn't the first time she'd pulled such a stunt. She knew what the end result would be. He would call and beg to come over. She would put him off, play with him, and then say, yes, hurry up, baby, baby.

Ellis was surprised to see Francine exit the community center so soon.

He had parked the car in the center's lot because he had spotted a couple others the same colors and size as his. Night had set in, and he doubted she would notice his car was occupied viewing it from the other side of the lot. He waited until Francine maneuvered the BMW out of the lot and made a right turn onto the street before he started his engine.

Royce had parked his dark green Pontiac down the block from the center under the beam of a street light. He was caught off guard even more by Francine's early return. Thinking he would be there for awhile, he had grabbed the latest Playboy magazine and began to go systematically through the pictorial sections. The magazine had fallen off the dashboard just as Francine was leaving the building. He had retrieved it, and then began pawing through the glove compartment, thinking it had to be cleaned out.

Royce looked up in time to see the BMW turn out the lot and start up the block. It was dark enough, and he was keyed up enough, that he didn't equate the Volvo that trailed Francine out of the parking lot with the black car that was between them all the way to the community center.

By the direction Francine was going Ellis thought she was on her way back home. She was taking a different route through a commercial district. Ellis guessed that she might stop and make a purchase.

Ellis never considered he might have someone tailing him until Royce was caught by a traffic light and had to speed up and cut through lanes to close the gap. After he viewed the Pontiac in the rear view mirror it dawned on him that he had seen the same car on the way to the community center. His suspicion was confirmed when Francine turned off the commercial street onto a residential block. The Pontiac fell right in behind them.

Ellis tried to figure out who could be tailing him, and for what reason. Nothing immediately came to mind. He pondered his list of options. He could let it go this time and look for the same thing to happen again, try to lose him, or go for a direct confrontation, even though he had no weapon.

When he reached a stop sign Ellis quickly clicked open his glove compartment and removed a six-inch long screwdriver. He slipped it into his jacket pocket.

As the trio of cars crossed an intersection a jeep maneuvered between Ellis' car and Royce's. Ellis seized the time to put his plan into action. He hit the gas, slowed, and swung his car up an empty driveway. Ellis let the in between car clear before backing sharply into the street and hitting the brakes. Ellis was already on his way out of his car as Royce's Pontiac jolted to a halt inches away from a collision. Ellis raced around to Royce on the driver's side, his right hand gripping the screwdriver in his jacket pocket as though it was a gun.

"What the fuck are you doing? Why are you following me?"

"I don't know what you mean," Royce said calmly. "I'm not following you."

"Like hell you're not. I oughta cap you!"

"Hey, don't mess up your nice jacket shooting at me. I'm just a little P.I trying to do his job."

"You're a private investigator?"

"Yeah."

Get out of the car."

"What for?"

"Just get the hell out of the car." Royce obeyed the order cautiously. "Take your I.D out slowly and hold it out to me."

Royce did as he was told again. Ellis came in close to read Royce's I.D in the dark.

"Brad Royce. Royce Investigations. I've heard of you. One of the biggest agencies in town. Guess what? I'm a private investigator too."

"You are. I thought you were a gangster out to rip me."

"Not with this thing." Ellis pulled the screwdriver from his jacket pocket. "An old P.I trick."

"I'm impressed."

"Ellis Mason. Mason Detective Agency."

"Nice to meet you."

"Who were you tailing if you weren't tailing me? Could it be Francine Darden?"

"Maybe. I can't say. Why were you tailing her?"

"Who says I was tailing her?"

"It looks like we have a stalemate."

Three cars had driven up behind those blocking the street. One driver was pushing hard on his car horn.

"We better clear out," Ellis said. "You never know who might be packing semi-automatic weapons these days."

Chapter 6

In the evening of the following day, Ellis and J.C found themselves at a table in a soul food diner that featured everything from New Orleans gumbo to down home drop biscuits. Ellis was with the woman he had been dating recently, Zoe. The new lady in J.C's life was called Loretta.

The foursome was sharing a bottle of wine while waiting for their meal to be delivered. Buxom and big-boned Loretta sipped from her glass and said:

"Ellis, J.C tells me you're responsible for turning his life around."

"I didn't do anything," Ellis said. "He did it all himself."

"I beg to differ with you, my man. You gave me a chance. A lotta people would've just turned their backs on an ex-con."

"You should be crediting your sister. She kept badgering me to hire you when you got paroled." Ellis smiled. "I was scared to tell her no because she has my files so screwed up I couldn't find anything if she ever got mad and quit."

"You can joke about it if you want. But you saved my life, brother. And I'll always appreciate it," J.C said sincerely.

Zoe smiled. "Oh, that's so sweet."

"If you guys don't stop it. We'll all be crying in a minute," Ellis said.

Sometime later, with dinner winding down, Ellis said:

"Are you going dancing with us?"

"Uh, I don't think so." J.C said. "Retta has to get up kinda early to go to work. So we gonna head on back to the crib and uh, you know, you know-"

"Play checkers," Loretta said.

"Play checkers."

Later, Ellis and Zoe were driving to a dance club located downtown.

"So what's happening with you?" Zoe asked.

"The same ol' same ol' at work. Except for one case. I checked out a girl friend for a client. And then she came up dead, and my client has been arrested for her murder."

"Damn. Do you think he did it?"

"Not yet I don't. He hired me to clear him if I can."

"Any luck?"

"Not yet."

Royce was in the living room of his father's house watching a Cub game on TV. They were downing beers and munching on corn chips. Mr. Royce was a more wrinkled, paunchier, gray haired version of Brad.

On the screen yet another bad thing happened to the Cubs. A pop fly was hit into short left field. Three Cub fielders went after the ball, but it landed between the trio for a hit. Since there were two outs, both runners on base scored, probably putting the game out of reach.

"Damn, they messed up another play," exclaimed Mr. Royce. "How do they keep doing it?"

"Easy. They're the Cubs. Nothing really good is ever gonna happen. We had sixty-nine. Goodbye nine game lead. Finally made the big jump to the play-offs in eighty-four. Win the first two games at home. And then bam. Lose three straight. No World Series at all. And the worst damn thing of all. The reason we didn't have three games at home. No lights in Wrigley Field. Cursed. The Cubs are cursed."

"Beautiful. Now you've depressed me. Hand me another beer."

Royce took a beer from the coffee table and handed it to his father.

Mr. Royce popped open his beer. "So. You working a big political case. I suppose you and Josh know what you're doing. I wouldn'tve taken the case myself. Of course, we didn't have dirty tricks in the old days. All you had to know was that you better not cross boss Daley too often. And I think the city was probably better off for it."

"But not detective agencies. By the time it's over we'll be taking in a pretty nice little fee."

The dance club was the type that catered to an eclectic mix of patrons from Armani wearing yuppies to generation Xers decked out in outlandish glitter outfits. The usual thumping disco beat was now being replaced by Smokey Robinson's slow tempo song, Just To See Her.

Ellis and Zoe were somewhere in the middle of the sea of humanity on the main dance floor. They were locked together in a tight embrace. Zoe, with her close cut brown hair that had a gerri curl glisten to it, had her head buried in Ellis' chest. She was a slender lightskinned woman with fashion model high cheekbones.

Ellis remembered a crude comment made by an old high school buddy. "If she lets you grab that booty, later on you can do your duty."

Ellis slid his hands down to Zoe's tight buns. When she didn't object he had a feeling he would be in for tonight.

To Ellis it seemed as though there was a quick cut to him being in his bedroom with a grip on Zoe's behind. He moved his left hand up and unzipped the back of her dress while planting a burning kiss on her lips. He helped Zoe slide her dress off her shoulders. Her only underwear was a pair of G-string panties.

Zoe slowly unbuttoned Ellis' shirt. They backed in the direction of the bed. Zoe made a final little leap that propelled them down upon the bed. She peppered his chest with kisses. Then she unfastened his pants and pulled the zipper downward. She only had to stroke him a few times before he reached a full erection. Zoe pivoted about, moving her rear end closer to Ellis.

"Tear 'em off me, " Zoe purred, Ellis gripped the waist band of her panties with both hands and ripped it apart. "Come on, baby. Abuse my butt."

Zoe parted her cheeks and landed perfectly on Ellis' rod. She bounced up and down, twisting her head from side to side.

"Sweet Jesus! I love getting kinky with you. I just love it!"

Ellis had been laying out letting Zoe do all the work. Now, he joined in rhythm with her bouncing actions, increasing the pace until he exploded with a burst.

Zoe eased upwards, reversed, and remounted Ellis. She leaned forward enough for him to tongue her breasts, going from one to the other. She was swept away when Ellis switched positions and plowed into her. She cried out and locked her legs tightly around his torso.

"Work me baby. Work me," Zoe moaned. "You're great. You're so great!"

Andrea sat at her desk going over surveillance photographs and time logs. Royce stood a few feet away gazing out of the office window. Royce tried to control himself, but couldn't resist periodically gazing in

Andrea's direction. He admired her shapely crossed legs, her three-quarter profile. Her only response was a quick, short smile.

"We're still following a paper trail on Miss Darden's apartment and car payments. Ryan's too smart to put it in his name. He's probably hiding it as a business expense through a dummy company."

"Probably." Andrea looked up from her papers. "You seem to have done a fine job. Thank you."

"No problem. Do you want us to stay on Ryan and Darden?"

"At the moment, no. We believe we have enough. But that may change at any time. So don't go away."

"I won't. Call me. Any time."

"I will."

Another short smile.

Chapter 7

J.C crossed the hall, rapped on Ellis' office door, and entered before getting permission. Ellis was hacking away on his computer.

"My homie. Came to pick up my check and deliver a message."

"I've got the check right here. What's the message?"

"My boy that's promoting the rap concert tonight called and said that the building is gonna have more doors open than metal detectors. They wondering how they gonna handle gangsters that wanna sneak in with a nine or something. So he wants you to be there, to, you know, supervise things."

"Aw man. I'm suppose to be on the Drew thing this evening."

"What you got to do? Tail that Darden babe again?"

"Yeah. I'm giving that one more try to see if it looks like she's up to something shady. Then I might just go straight to her and see what she has to say."

"Hey. I'll tell you what. You can handle the concert thing, and I'll tail the babe. Ain't no big thing. I'll nail it."

Ellis leaned back in his chair. "Yeah. I guess we better do it that way."

Francine entered her bedroom dressed in her work outfit. She looked at herself in the circular dresser mirror.

"Girl, you looking too square."

She made a move to change that. She removed her pinstriped suit jacket and tossed it over her shoulder onto the bed. She undid her black string tie and unbuttoned her white cotton blouse. Next she wiggled out of her skirt. Francine tossed her blouse, undid her strapless bra, letting it fall to the floor. She placed her left hand on the dresser top as she slipped out of her panties.

Francine did a 180 in the mirror and glanced back over her shoulder.

"You're a hot babe. No wonder so many guys are hot for my twat."

She stroked her curly patch of pubic hair and laughed.

She was in one of her wild wicked moods. The kind that made her attend Ryan's public appearances just to tease him, fawn over him like a typical political groupie, approach his wife and make small talk, catch him alone and whisper something nasty in his ear.

Francine did a little dance in front of the mirror. She thought maybe she should go to the fund-raiser buck naked. That would really make her a star.

The fund raising dinner for Ryan was being held in a ballroom of a chain hotel located in a Northwest suburb of Chicago. Politicians, journalists, celebrities, sports figures, and just plain old rich folks were present.

Francine glided into the room dressed in a strapless clinging black number that had a slit up the middle. creating a triangle effect. She scanned the room and recognized several of the faces. Some were politicians she had been with. She would speak to some. Others she would kill if she thought she could get away with it.

Ryan was up near the front where the podium set up was located. A group of six, including Ryan's wife, were conversing among themselves, some sipping from drinks.

Francine sauntered forward, staring in Ryan's direction. He made eye contact with her, and then quickly darted his eyes away, more out of embarrassment than lust. Sensing this made her whirl about and put her back to him. She contemplated an early exit until she noticed someone who had just walked in.

He was a tall cute-handsome man in his early thirties with a big head of boutique styled hair. His name was Mark Carbo, a TV reporter new in town.

The first time Francine saw Carbo on the air she was sitting up in bed after taking a shower. She was so turned on by him that she got herself off and had a big time orgasm. She was feeling that way now.

Francine deliberately moved in Carbo's direction. Before she could reach him he turned and stepped out into a hall. She hesitated before following him. Twenty feet down from her Carbo was talking with a guy lugging around a mini-cam. When the camera moved away she quickly approached him.

"Hi. Are you who I think you are?"

"I don't know. Who do you think I am?"

"Mark Carbo. The TV reporter."

"You're right on target."

"I bet you're here to cover Congressman Ryan."

"Right again."

"How long will you be here?"

"Just to get the speech on tape. And do a stand up. I won't stay for dinner."

"Maybe I could help you with the dinner thing."

"Probably not. I'll have to get back to the station."

"Well. Maybe some other time. I'm Francine Darden."

J.C sat alone in his battered Buick listening to jazz music with the sound turned down low. He was parked in the lot of a steak house Francine had driven to after leaving the site of the fund raising dinner.

J.C would rather be listening to hip-hop music, but he believed if you can't play hip-hop loud, you don't need to play it at all.

Ten minutes later he watched Francine come into the lot and move to her BMW. He gave her ten-second head start before following her out into the street. He tailed her the two blocks to interstate I-41. Just inside the city limits Francine turned her car off the road and pulled it into a motel court.

The motel was L-shaped with double deck cabins and black iron stairs leading to the second deck.

When J.C saw Francine park her car near the separate motel office he pulled in next to a used car lot. On the front seat next to him were a pair of binoculars and an infra red camera with a long lense attachment. He used the camera to snap several photos of Francine climbing the stairs and moving toward a cabin after exiting her car. He watched her do something at the cabin door before unlocking it and disappearing inside. He peered through the binoculars and saw that Francine had tied a yellow ribbon around the doorknob.

"What are you up to baby?" he asked himself.

J.C had listened to back to back Miles Davis tunes by the time a red Corvette pulled into the motel court, bypassing the office. A thin man of average height with a head of unruly dark red hair emerged from the car. He scoped the cabins before heading in the direction of the cabin with the ribbon on the door.

J.C was caught off guard and didn't realize that the man was on his way to Francine's room. He got in so easily J.C never had a chance to get a good angle for a photograph.

"Damn. I'll catch your ass coming out."

Starting his car, J.C drove into the motel court, positioning himself in a spot to get a great view of Francine's room.

Francine had been pacing about in a semi-circle when Benny Carr entered the room.

"How you doing sweet thing," Benny said, flashing a smile that lit up his craggy face. "You look damn good. Good enough to eat for dinner."

"Forget about that. I'm not nearly in the mood."

"I'm really starting to get worried about, you know, Donna getting killed."

"What's to worry about? Her old man popped her."

"Suppose the police are wrong. Suppose somebody else did it."

"What makes you think that?"

Francine brushed the hair from in front of her face. "I've been. I have the feeling like maybe somebody has been following me."

Benny stepped forward and placed his hand on her shoulder. "I think you're just being a little paranoid. Just relax. Things are cool."

Benny planted a kiss on Francine's cheek

Unexpected complications. They can happen in the lives of just about anybody, even a hired assassin. A revelation had come to the man seated alone in the car parked at the edge of a gas station court. It was no coincidence that the car that had been between him and Francine's car had stopped near the used car lot in front of him. The fact that he moved to the motel court after the guy had gone into Francine's room confirmed him as a player in the game. How or why he didn't know. In fact, he didn't care.

The assassin had made up his mind. The motel was a prime target area. It bothered him a little that he would have to perform a three for one hit, but business was business, work was work.

He started the engine, not bothering to turn on the headlights. He drove past the used car lot and motel court to a spot along the shoulder and beyond the motel office. He parked the car and stepped into the cool night air.

He was at least six feet tall. He wore a full-length trench coat. His right hand was hidden in his coat pocket.

The assassin walked casually into the motel court. Without being obvious he checked to see if anyone was watching him. All clear. He picked up his pace when he was within ten feet of J.C's car. From the pocket of his trench coat, off a couple special made hooks, he took a .32 automatic with a silencer attached. With a quick motion, before J.C had time to react, the assassin took aim and shot through the car windshield. The bullet caught J.C in the temple. He fell sideways and landed on the cushioned seat. The assassin stuck the silencer through the circular hole left by the bullet and shot J.C in the head a second time.

After a quick scan of the area looking for witnesses, the assassin returned the gun to his pocket and casually walked back to his car. Inside, he checked his watch. Three minutes. That's how long he would wait. Give them time to start going at it hot and heavy. Then he would make his move.

The assassin's plan came tumbling down a minute and a half later. It began when the door to a first floor cabin near the front of the L shaped row came flying open. A Hispanic woman in her twenties rushed out. She was wearing only a pair of panties. She used an article of clothing to cover breasts.

"Help me! Somebody help me!" the woman cried.

She ran in the direction of the motel office.

"Come back here, you worthless bitch!" shouted a paunchy man in his underwear.

A clerk from the office raced out into the night. Curious onlookers from other cabins came into view.

The assassin knew it was all over. He would have to leave before the police arrived.

Chapter 8

Ellis was in bed asleep. The ringing phone stirred him. He reached over and lifted the receiver.

"Yeah. Hello."

"Is this Ellis Mason?"

"Yeah."

"I'm Lieutenant Russo. Homicide. Do you know J.C Connors? Is he am employee of your's?"

Ellis' head cleared and he became more alert. "Yeah. Has something happened?"

"I have some bad news for you, Mr. Mason. J.C Connors has been murdered."

Ellis was stunned. "Aw man. No. Are you sure?"

"Pretty much. Yes. The body was found in his car. His ID was present on his person. We're here downtown. We'd like you to come in and speak with us when you can."

"Yeah. Okay. I guess I can come in now. You know, as soon as I can get there."

"All right. Thank you for your co-operation."

Ellis suddenly felt weighed down by any kind of movement. It was a struggle for him to make it out of bed. His mind was scattered. Get dressed. Take a bath. Get your pants on. Take a shower. Put on your shoes. He calmed enough to change into the clothes he had worn the night before. He sprayed on some deodorant and gathered his car keys.

If he was ever asked Ellis wouldn't be able to tell anyone how he made it to police headquarters. He somehow landed in a small dingy office with Lt. Russo, a beer bellied man with a brush-like mustache and thinning hair. His partner was Sergeant Boulware, a tall thin black guy in his forties. He had salt and pepper hair and a full beard.

Ellis sat near the desk with Boulware. Russo faced them with his back against the wall.

"Let's see where we should start here," Boulware said. "With the camera and binoculars found in his car, wasn't Mr. Connors working tonight?"

"Yes. He was working on a routine divorce case."

"He was tailing a subject and taking photographs, am I right?"

"What's this subject's name?"

"Francine Darden."

Boulware said: "What does she look like? The body was found after answering a domestic disturbance call at the motel. The officers on the scene saw shattered glass from the car windshield."

"She's good looking. Blonde. Shapely. In her twenties."

"Maybe the motel owner will remember her. I doubt if she used her real name."

"Nothing was taken," Russo said. "Robbery wasn't the motive for the shooting. Tell us about your client. And the divorce case."

"I can't do that. It's privileged information."

"Bull shit!" snarled Russo. He came forward and lorded over Ellis. "You know, I really hate it when you P.Is pull this crap. We've got a murder case here, for God's sake. It's your partner. I guess he was your friend. You jack us around like this, and I'll try to get whatever little license you have suspended. Do you hear me jack-"

Boulware leaned forward. "Hold on now. Let's not lose it here. I'm sure Mr. Mason is distraught over the lost of his associate. I'm sure he'll co-operate once he has time to mull things over." He took a card from a desk drawer and handed it to Ellis. "Call us when you have something. Of course, we might get back to you."

In his car, Ellis felt thankful that Boulware had let him off the hook. Unless they were playing good cop, bad cop, he figured Russo would've wanted to badger and intimidate him into revealing what he knew. Or maybe they both figured they would need his help to solve the case. The state of mind Ellis was in made him believe he had the best chance of finding the person that murdered J.C.

The following morning, driving in his car, Ellis was feeling somewhat better. Partly because he had gotten in contact with Royce, and he had agreed to meet with him.

Other thoughts flashed through Ellis' mind. He recalled stopping by Maybeline's house after leaving the police station. Other relatives and friends were already there. He would never forget the look of supreme anguish he saw on Maybeline's face as he approached her. He had wanted to say just the right things to her, but the words never came. All he could do was hold onto her as tightly as possible.

Ellis stepped into the office complex of Royce Investigations. A receptionist was there to greet him. She gave him the directions to Royce's office.

As he moved through a spacious workroom Michelle Grant was coming toward him. He found himself turning and watching her move away.

When Ellis entered Royce's office Royce came to his feet and shook hands with him.

"Hey. Nice to see you again. Under different circumstances."

"Yeah. This is some layout you have here. Very impressive."

"Thanks. Have a seat." Ellis sat in one of the chairs opposite the desk. "Now what is this with Francine Darden?"

Ellis told Royce about Armad hiring him to keep tabs on Donna Beck, her murder, and Armad being charged with the crime.

"And uh. Something bad happened last night. I sent a guy out to tail Francine Darden. He followed her to a motel. Somebody shot him while he was sitting in his car." Ellis became more emotional than he wanted to be. "I brought the kid into the business. I thought I was turning his life around. I was. I was suppose to be out there last night. But we ended up switching assignments. Aw man. It's a crazy world out in them streets."

"Yeah. Yeah."

Ellis ran his hand across his eyes. "I don't believe it was a screwed up robbery attempt. Or somebody that had a beef with J.C. I think it's tied to Miss Darden's activities. Did it ever appear to you that she was involved in anything illegal?"

"Not at all. I'm not supposed to tell you this. The reason the agency was investigating her is uh, politically motivated. More of a personal relationship thing than a crime-related."

"Damn. I guess what I need to do is get inside her place and look around for anything incriminating. But it's a security building. I'll never even get in."

Royce took a deep breath. I'm sorry about what happened to your associate. Maybe I can help you out a little bit. There's a way we can get into her apartment. It may take a couple hours or so to get the operation rolling."

The key to Royce's plan was a van that had the same colors as those driven by Illinois Bell employees. They also wore the same color and type of work uniform.

The van eventually parked just far enough down the block for the building's doorman to see, but not close enough for him to identify the logo.

In their fake uniforms, Ellis and Royce entered the vestibule of Francine's building. Royce carried a clipboard, Ellis a black satchel.

"Good morning gentlemen," the doorman said. "How may I help you?"

"We're with Illinois Bell. We have a job to do." Royce gazed at the clipboard. "For a Miss Francine Darden."

"Yes. I know her. I'm sure she's at work right now."

"Is there a janitor or manager that can let us in?"

"The janitor could be anywhere. But the manager is in room 101."

In the elevator, Ellis said: "You nailed it, man. You pretty smooth."

"I try to be."

They left the elevator and searched out apartment 101. A middle-aged woman with curly blue hair answered their knock.

"Good morning, ma'am," Royce said pleasantly. "We're with the phone company. We'll need to gain entry to a tenant's apartment. A Miss Francine Darden."

"Yes. But I'm sure she's not home right now."

"Actually, that would be better." Royce spoke softer. "You see. We have reason to believe Miss Darden may be using a device that cheats the company out of money we so richly deserve."

"Oh my God! She seems so nice."

"The real crooks always do. What we need to do is give us a passkey so we can thoroughly check things out. And of course, keep this only between us."

"Oh certainly. I can do that."

Royce was the first one to enter Francine's apartment after unlocking the door with a passkey. Ellis followed him in and re-locked the door behind him.

"Not bad for a secretary, huh," Ellis said.

"No. You can start here. I'll take the bedroom."

Royce exited the room.

Ellis started at a telephone table. He searched out an address book. It was loaded with names. He crossed the room to a fake fireplace. A pair of vases rested on the mantle. Ellis looked inside the two vases. Nothing. Along one of the walls was a bookcase. There were paperbacks, hard covers, and magazines. Trashy novels, romance novels. Business, computer, and modeling books. The magazines were mostly fashion. A few businesses and finance publications were thrown in.

At random Ellis picked out a fashion magazine. As he thumped through it a collection of papers fell out onto the floor. Ellis scooped them up. They were campaign stickers and literature from Ryan's camp. The edge of a photo jutted from a booklet. He pulled it free. In the photo Francine was pictured with Ryan. She had her arms around his shoulder. She was wearing an evening gown, he a tux. From the background they appeared to be at a campaign event.

Simultaneously, Royce went through Francine's bedroom. He began by going to the closet and discovering what he expected. Expensive clothing of all types. He checked a jewelry box that was on the dresser. Some real stuff. Some fake. Nice looking pearls. Small carat diamond rings. Next he went to the dresser drawers. Nothing in the top drawers. In the second drawer he came up with a metal storage box. He figured it could contain important papers, even secret ones. It was locked. Royce returned it to the drawer because he was afraid Ellis would want to force it open, a move that would tip Francine that someone had been there.

In the corner of the next drawer Royce uncovered a bankbook from a big chain. The balance was twenty thousand dollars.

Ellis entered the room carrying the address book, Ryan photo, and campaign literature.

"Did you scope out anything?"

"What you would expect. Fancy clothes and some nice jewelry. I did get a bankbook. A 20K balance."

"Any big withdrawals or deposits?"

"No. Just a steady stream of deposits. Eight hundred to a thousand dollars every six weeks or so."

Ellis held up the address book. "I've got an address book filled with names. If I take it, she'll probably think she lost it around the house somewhere."

"We don't need to risk it." Royce reached into the pocket of his shirt. He removed a miniature camera. "Let me have the book. I'll photograph every page."

"You're like the boy scouts. Always prepared."

"I try to be."

Royce took the address book and placed it on the dresser top. He began snapping photographs of each page.

Ellis moved in the direction of the dresser. "I found some campaign literature in the living room. From Congressman Ryan." He held up the picture of Ryan and Francine. "I have a feeling Mr. Ryan is playing daddy money bags to Miss Darden. Am I right?"

Royce hesitated before answering. "You're quicker than what I thought you were."

"We've got sex, money, and maybe some pillow talking. That can be a lethal combination."

"Yeah. But we don't have any evidence that's the case."

"Not yet. But if it's there, I'll find it."

Chapter 9

Ryan and Dan North, a fiftish guy at least forty pounds heavier than Ryan, sat across from each other at the table in Ryan's office. North was Ryan's long time campaign manager.

Ryan was munching on a fish sandwich. North had a greasy burger and a Coors beer.

"So, how do you like the idea? How do you like the plan?"

Ryan stopped chewing his sandwich. "I don't. Politics is suffering from this kind of behavior."

"And you'll be suffering if you don't fight fire with fire." North took a swig from his beer. "The Republicans started it sixteen years ago. You know, it blew up in their faces with the Watergate thing. But they're still pulling the dirty tricks thing. You can believe they have something planned for you."

"You have a point there."

"What we'd be doing wouldn't even count as a real dirty trick. It's just that we could have an in to Cody's organization if you want to take it. They're looking for paid temp workers. We've got a couple overqualified ladies that could easily get hired. And then we'd have a spy inside Cody's organization."

"Let me say this. I still don't like this kinda thing. But since you've got it all set up, you might as well go on with it."

Royce was seated across from Marty Silver at his desk. Adrea stood near the window with her arms folded. She was wearing a skirt several inches above her knee. Royce was finding it hard to keep his eyes off her legs.

"What I have is a connection between Miss Darden and a murder."

"Murder, That's amazing. How did it come about?" Silver asked.

"I just picked up a little bit of info from another P.I. She knows a murder victim. And this guy's client seems to think she and Miss Darden might have been into something on the illegal side."

"Illegal enough to cause murder."

"It's really only a theory at this point," Royce said. "It's nothing concrete."

"My God, if it pans out, we could drop an atomic bomb when the time is right."

"I assume you want me to reactivate in terms of Miss Darden."

"Most certainly."

"You're doing a fine job," Andrea said in a deadpan tone followed by a quick smile.

"Thanks."

Royce let his eyes linger on Andrea longer than he meant to. He went from her face down to her legs. Since the break up of his last relationship he had put women on the back burner of his life. He was beginning to think he was ready again. He knew he probably had no chance with Andrea, but there were at least a couple million women in the Chicago area just waiting to feel his fire.

Chapter 10

Armad had been transferred to Cook County Jail. Ellis met with him in a jail visiting area. Although he was on the "free" side of the glass, Ellis could feel the aura of forced confinement that seemed to be dancing through the air he breathed.

"My brother, I thought you had forgot about me," Armad said after sitting across from Ellis. "I thought you might've took the money and ran."

"No. I've been working."

"Have you got some good news for me?"

"I have some bad. I lost a partner. He was killed in his car while he was tailing Francine."

"Aw man, that's tough," Armad said sincerely. "How old was the man?"

"Twenty-three, twenty-four, twenty-five. Damn. I can't get it straight in my mind."

"In some places in the hood that's a long life. It shouldn't be that way, though. It took me a long time to figure that out. And now here I am jammed up on a bogus murder charge. Do you know how it went down?"

"He was shot through the windshield. No money was taken. I don't think it was a pay back thing. So that leaves a possible connection to Francine. And I don't know where that is. Do you have any ideas?"

"Don't know. Didn't nobody hear or see anything?"

"No. Not even the shots."

"That don't seem right."

"It was near a motel. They could've been playing TVs, radios, or whatever."

Armad nodded his head. "Yeah, Yeah. Maybe the killer was a stone cold gangster. And he had a piece with a silencer. And that's why nobody heard anything. He could've made your man and wanted to cap him for some reason."

"Could be. Let me ask you this. We did a background check on Donna Beck. She was from a pretty tough neighborhood on the South side. Did she still hang with anybody from her old neighborhood? Anybody that had done any time?"

"Yeah. There was one brother. His name is Zeke Wilson. You know, in high school they had one of them first time love-sex thangs. When you think you in love, and the sex is hot and heavy. So you still remember 'em even after you break up. They used to run into each other at clubs. Or like when somebody they knew got married."

"You ever get to know him?" Ellis asked.

"Naw. Not really. I talked to him at a bar a few times. Sometimes he would be with this big ol' biker looking white boy he met in the joint."

"You know his name?"

"Not his first name. They call him Mongo. His last name is Pike, I believe."

"Well, I guess that's it for now. I'll check back with you later."

Ellis stood up to leave.

"Hey man. Tell the truth, do you really believe I didn't do it?"

"To tell the truth. As long as your case is tied to what happened to J.C, I'll be all over it."

Ellis found himself returning to Royce Investigations. The same Midwest version of a valley girl was working the reception area.

"Hello. How may I help you?"

"Hi. Do you remember me from before? I'm Ellis Mason."

"Oh yeah. I'm sure. Like I always remember really cute, slightly older guys."

"I'm still working on a case with Mr. Royce. Can you direct me to your computer data banks?"

"Oh sure. Just go two doors down and turn to your left. If you'd like, I'll buzz them 'em and tell 'em you're on the way."

"Okay."

The computer center contained four personal computers resting on separate small desk. Along the walls was a quartet of chest-like data bank storage computers. Two women and a man were working at the PCs. Michelle Grant was one of the women.

Ellis entered the area. He recognized Michelle as the hot brown babe with braids that he had seen the day before. He approached her.

"Hi. I'm-"

"Ellis Mason. Michelle Grant. How may I help you?"

Ellis took a small strip of paper from his pocket. "I need a criminal background check on two men. Most of their records are probably in

Illinois."

Michelle looked at the paper. "I can request a criminal background check. I may get something from the Parole Board or department of Corrections."

Ellis watched Michelle start to hack. From behind a male voice said:

"What the hell is going on here?"

Ellis turned about and saw Royce in an agitated state.

"Oh. Hey, I have a couple new leads. I need to little help getting a run down on them."

Royce moved all the way over to Ellis. "What are you doing? I felt bad about your partner and I helped you out. But that doesn't give you license to use my facilities without my permission. Especially when you deceive my receptionist."

"Hey. I just took a page from your book. But if you pissed off, I can cut. I'll pick up the info somewhere else. Even though the info will help your client. I'm guessing it's that Cody guy."

Ellis turned and started to leave.

"Wait a minute," Royce said. "What have you got?"

"The names of two men with records that knew Donna Beck. If they knew Donna, they might know Francine too. If you get tie to a murder, the scandal will blow up even larger when it's leaked to the public. Am I right?"

"You're right," Royce said. "Let's get out of here and let Michelle do her work."

CRIMINAL ACTIVITY FILE: Zeke Wilson. Male black. Age 26.

JUVENILE RECORD: Convictions; car theft-2. Burglary. ADULT RECORD:

Arrested for Assault and Battery twice. Conviction; 1982. Served nine months. Questioned in connection with illegal lottery operation. No arrest ever made. Conviction; 1985. Served 21 months for Involuntary Manslaughter.

CRIMINAL ACTIVITY FILE: William "Mongo" Pike. Male white. Age 29. No Juvenile record. Arrested for Assault. Charges later dropped. Arrested three times in drug sweeps. Never charged with a crime. Questioned in connection with a contract killing. Never charged with a crime. Conviction; 1985. Served nine months for credit card fraud.

   "They're some pair, huh," Royce said after they had examined the printouts.

   "Yeah. All I have to do is find a connection and act on it. If it's one that can be acted on."

   Ellis made a move to exit.

   "Hey, I'm sorry I blew up at you a little," Royce said.

   "Don't sweat it man. I was a little overzealous. I'm just. I want who killed J.C so bad I can taste it. I have to get them before the trail gets cold."

Chapter 11

Along with the other background information, Ellis picked up a last known address for Zeke Wilson. He climbed the stairs of the three-story walk up after ringing a buzzer in the vestibule. In the old days people would be waiting on you by the time you made it up the stairs. These days it wasn't such a good idea.

Ellis reached the top of the stairs and turned to the right. He banged on the burglar bars that fronted a second wooden door. A few seconds later a black woman in her fifties with heavy lines in her face cracked the door open.

"Yeah."

"How you doing? I rang the buzzer. I'm looking for Zeke Wilson. Does he still live here?"

"Who are you? Are you with the police? Or that parole thang?"

"Ma'am. I'm going to tell you the truth. I'm a private investigator." Ellis removed his ID and held it up for the woman to see. "Mr. Wilson may be able to help me locate a missing person. Is he around?"

"No. He's not."

"You can help me out if you let me know when he comes back here."

"Why the hell should I help you? Nobody does a goddamn thang for me."

"You know what they say, ma'am. What goes around comes around."

Ellis made a move to leave.

"Wait a minute. Maybe I'll help you out a little. Have you got a phone number?"

Ellis went back and handed the woman a business card through the bars. "Thank you ma'am. I appreciate it."

Ellis descended the stairs. He wasn't sure if the woman would really help him or not. At least he knew a place Wilson could be found.

Mrs. Ryan, a portrait of the typical TV sit-com wife, came down the stairs and answered the ringing phone.

"Hello."

"Hi. Is Wal-, uh Congressman Ryan home?"

"Yes he is. Honey, telephone," she called out.

Ryan entered the room from the kitchen. "Who is it?"

"A woman. Probably from the campaign office."

Mrs. Ryan handed the receiver to her husband. She left the room through the doorway leading to the kitchen.

"Hello. Ryan here."

"Hi. It's me. Where have you been?" Francine asked with a mix of scorn and concern.

Ryan glanced toward the hallway and skipped over to the other side of the room. "I told you not to call me here. Why did you do it now?"

"Where the hell have you been? You've never pushed me away before. You're dumping me, aren't you? Just in time for your stupid-assed election!"

"What is wrong with you?" Ryan whispered loudly. "You're not making any sense."

"Fuck you, fuck you, fuck you!"

"This is pointless. I'm hanging up."

Ryan took a deep breath and put the receiver back in place.

In her apartment, Francine began to cry as soon as she hung up the phone. Tears seemed to flow down her face in a never-ending supply.

Her mind was filled with thoughts of lost hope and broken dreams. The luxury she lived in could no longer ease her troubled mind. She felt as if the walls of the apartment were closing in on her.

Francine raced into the bathroom. She turned on the wash basin faucet and splashed water on her face. She looked at herself in the medicine cabinet mirror and wondered who the hell she was.

Francine came into the bedroom. She bee-lined to the closet. She had to search way in the back to find what she was looking for.

Wearing a virginal white dress with a high collar and an above the kneecap hemline, Francine left her building and moved to the parking lot. Once she was in her BMW, she hit Lake Shore Drive and headed South. She made a turn and went west. At a traffic light, the flow of tears returned. She had to blink and wipe her eyes in order to see the road when the light changed.

Before she realized it, Francine had drifted to Bridgeport, the neighborhood she lived in when she first came to town. The four story dark brown apartment building located on a corner was where she had resided.

Francine parked her car a few feet down from the intersection. She entered the building.

Royce had followed Francine from home to the building. When he saw the BMW park he had pulled over to the curb on the other side of the intersection. He wondered why she had stopped at such a place. To visit a co-worker? A friend? Or maybe to buy drugs?

Actually, Royce was growing weary of tailing Francine. He was in favor of confronting her and attempting to get her to willingly come over to their side. He still hadn't run the idea by Cody and Andrea. He made a mental note to do it tomorrow.

As he sat there in the dark he caught an eyeful of a shapely babe in a pair of Daisy duke cut off jeans. Royce faced the front again and witnessed a sight that made his heart do a dance. Francine was on the roof of the building standing very close to the edge. Her white dress against the dark sky created the illusion of an angel ready to take flight, but this angel didn't have wings.

Royce left his car and raced up the block toward the corner. No cars were passing. He stopped in the middle of the street, gazing upward at Francine.

"Hey lady. You better watch out. You might fall. Lady!"

Initially, Francine seemed oblivious to Royce's words. She suddenly whirled about and ran toward the middle of the roof.

Royce backpedaled to get a better view of the roof. In a flash of white he saw Francine disappear through a roof door. He crossed the street thinking she would be down soon. Three minutes passed. He decided to return to his car. Inside, he punched out a number on his car phone.

"Hello."

"Yeah. It's Royce. Are you at home now?"

"Yeah. What's up?"

"Something weird just went down. I tailed Francine to a building in Bridgeport. She acted like she was going to jump. I scared her off. But now she's made me. I don't know what she might have in her head. I need you to come down here and be ready to tail her when she leaves."

"She's still there. Why are you calling me instead of your guys?"

"I remembered your address. You're the closest. If you're coming, hurry up. I'm in a black 83 Mustang. If I'm gone, you'll know I had to pick her up."

"Give me the address and I'll be right there."

The wait wasn't that long, it just seemed that way to Royce. He checked his rear view mirror when a car pulled in behind his. There was a wave and a touch of the car horn. Royce exited his car and moved back to Ellis'.

"What took you so long?"

Ellis scooted to the middle of the seat. "I didn't take long. Is she still inside?"

"Yeah. I guess she'll be out in a second."

"Suppose she got inside somebody's apartment. And now she's in the bathroom about to slit her wrists."

"You know how to be morbid, don't you? Maybe one of us should go in and look for her."

"In this neighborhood it better be you."

Royce never had the chance to move. Francine walked slowly from the building to her car. He darted behind a nearby tree. He waved goodbye to Ellis.

Ellis entered the bar and made a snap evaluation. It seemed to be a cross between a typical blue-collar neighborhood bar and a singles and couples hang out. Over twenty-one to fifty type couples were scattered about the tables and counter. Unescorted men and women were also present.

Ellis had raised the black population of the bar to exactly one. From the stares he was getting reaching number one wasn't exactly an every day occurrence. He ignored the attention and moved to table in a far corner.

Francine was seated at the bar on a stool nursing a drink. She obviously was in a down cast mood. She finished the drink before her in one big gulp, and then asked for another.

Ten minutes passed before a waitress wandered over to Ellis' table. He rewarded her by ordering their cheapest size of beer. By then one man had made his sway to the counter next to Francine. He was quickly shot down and sent packing.

After six minutes Ellis' beer was delivered to him. He sipped from it and watched another guy take a shot at Francine. The second guy was repelled faster than the first.

Francine downed three more shots of bourbon. Ellis was worried about her going to the john and deciding to hurt herself. He would have a hard time explaining why he had to go rushing into the ladies room.

It became a moot point when Francine paid her tab. With a lost expression on her face, she slowly trekked toward the door.

Instinctively, Ellis made the snap decision to go after her and make contact. Tell her who he was and why he was shadowing her. Anything to break her mood. Anything to get her home safely, or to a friend she could talk to.

Ellis made it to the ten to twelve foot vestibule that led to the bar just as Francine was stepping outside. He heard a pair of popping sounds followed by the screech of car tires. He raced forward, blasting through the door into the street. He saw Francine lying on the sidewalk. Keyed on the dark blue late model Chevy as it thundered to the end of the block and made a sharp left turn. He ran after the car trying to get a good look at the license plate. No such luck.

Ellis returned to Francine. She was lying on her back with her arms outstretched. The angle of her head was turned mostly to the left. The damage had been done to the right side of her face. A bullet had ripped through it, sending blood and chunks of flesh flying. Her right eye had been jolted from its socket. He didn't bother to check for vital signs. He knew she was dead.

"Jesus have mercy." Ellis moved to the door and opened it. "Hey! Somebody's been shot. Call the police. Call the police!"

The bar's burly bartender came on the scene. "My God! What the hell happened?"

"She was hit in a drive by."

"The police are on the way. Gee, shouldn't we cover her up or something?"

"Not until the police get here. Do you know her?"

"No."

Over half the patrons from the bar stepped out and viewed the horrific murder scene before scurrying away. Ellis saw no reason to try and stop them. The typical group of morbidly curious onlookers arrived on the scene. Ellis and the bartender did their best to keep them clear of the crime location.

Standing on the street, after glancing over at the body, it dawned on Ellis that not only was life unfair, but so was death. You get gunned down in the street. And then you have to lay there with your face erased while a bunch of strangers gawked at you.

A pair of police patrol cars arrived within a few seconds of each other. The patrolmen interviewed Ellis about what he saw. They didn't ask. And he didn't volunteer to tell them he was a private investigator tailing the dead woman. They asked him to stay until Homicide detectives arrived.

Ellis realized it just wasn't going to be his night when the assigned detectives made their appearance. One was a frizzy-haired woman in jeans and a red Bulls starter jacket. Boulware was the other.

"What have we got here?" Boulware asked a uniformed cop.

"A drive by shooting. A witness that saw the car get away."

"Have you IDed her yet?"

"She had a wallet in her dress pocket. Her name is Francine Darden."

"Damn. I know that name." As he approached the bar Boulware recognized Ellis.

"The black guy over there. Is he the witness?"

"Yeah."

"You know him?"

"Yeah." Boulware reached the spot outside the roped off area where Ellis was standing. "Mr. Mason."

"Sgt. Boulware."

"Follow me. We've got some serious talking to do."

Boulware led Ellis back to his car. He opened the rear door and let Ellis in first. He followed him.

"Okay, my man. I helped you out when Russo was all over your ass. Now you gotta do something for me. You partner gets killed tailing a woman. And now the woman is shot down in the street. What the fuck is going on, man?"

"I wish I knew."

"Take a stab at it for me," Boulware urged.

"You might not like all of this. But here goes. I was hired by a man that's sitting in jail for the recent murder of Donna Beck. He says he didn't do it. He turned me onto Francine Darden as possibly being involved in something shady with Donna Beck."

"Have you uncovered anything?"

"No."

"So are you saying the three murders are connected?"

"Maybe. Uh. J.C getting shot while tailing Francine. After tonight. Maybe he was standing between a clear shot at somebody capping Francine. But then again, maybe my client killed Donna. A robber killed R.C, and a crazy-assed son of a bitch took a random pot shot at Francine. I don't know. I'm just a small businessman. I do security at concerts. I'm no expert at this."

"I'm glad you said that. You're better off staying out of an active murder case. Will you promise me that?"

Ellis looked away and then back at Boulware. "I can't. The kid was only twenty-four. I sent him out there and somebody took his life away. I just can't let it go."

"All right. I helped you out once. Don't expect it again if you get your ass in a sling."

Chapter 12

Silver, Andrea, Cody, and Brooks were assembled at the conference table in Cody's office.

"We've received the results of our latest poll," Silver said. "We trail Ryan by only eight percentage points. This is excellent. This is better than we hoped for at this point in the campaign."

"Perhaps this would be an opportune time to unleash our scandal info on Ryan's kept mistress," Andrea suggested.

"Have you decided how it should be done?" Cody asked.

"Yes. King at the Tribune is our best bet," Silver said. "Of course, the information won't come directly to him. His girl Friday will get it from an unknown source."

"I don't know. I'm starting to have second thoughts about this entire operation," Brooks said.

Andrea turned her attention to Cody. "It's your call. But let me add this. The voters, especially women, seem to be against candidate's personal sleaze this election year. Witness what occurred with Gary Hart."

"You've got a point there." Cody tapped the table top repeatedly with his fingertips. "But then again, all is fair in politics. Just so it doesn't get traced back to me."

Royce and Ellis were standing at the window in Royce's office gazing at the Chicago skyline.

"If it's one thing they can do in this town, that's put up some fantastic buildings," Royce said.

"Yeah."

"So. It looks like our cases have been thrown for a loop by this murder. I always wanted to work a Bogart type case. But now?"

"I guess it'll be a little harder to blow open a mistress scandal when the mistress has just been murdered."

"You got it."

I bet Cody and his people aren't so happy right about now."

"They might not know. I'll have to check and see." Royce put his back to the window. "How does the latest murder change your way of thinking?"

"I'm starting to think my client may not be playing me. Look at it this way. What do Donna Beck and Francine Darden have in common? They worked at the same brokerage firm. They were friends. And they were murdered within days of each other. All these things can't be coincidence."

"It doesn't seem like it."

"But on the other hand. Francine was in a strange mental state. She could've been laying some threats on Ryan. Maybe she became a liability they couldn't afford to deal with."

"I'm not with you on that angle. Politics in rough and dirty, but I don't think it's gotten that dirty yet."

"Maybe not. I'm just reaching and grabbing. I'm not sure what the hell I should do next."

Royce moved to his desk and leaned against the edge. "We picked up a little something from the photographs we took of Miss Darden's address book. She had two numbers written down without a name. We used a contact to cross check it and come up with a name and address. One of them belonged to Andrea Newsome. She works for a political consultant. Marty Silver. Silver is part of Cody's campaign."

"Aw man. Damn. Did they know about the Darden-Ryan connection?"

"Yeah."

"Did she mention that she knew Francine Darden?"

"No."

Ellis paced about in a semi-circle. "Is that strange to you? Maybe she had something going with Donna and Francine."

"You're really stretching it now. Miss Newsome is a highly paid, competent professional woman. What reason would she have to do anything illegal?"

"Come on man. Get real. Every time you look around some guy Reagan appointed is in some kind of trouble for some shady dealings. They were highly paid professionals."

"Yeah. But shady business practices are not nearly the same as murder."

"It'll probably be the next big step in the sleaze factor that's taking over the country."

"Man. How did we get side tracked onto this?" Royce asked. "All I'm saying is it's unlikely they even know each other. Francine may have found out Silver was working with Cody and wrote the number down. She probably never even used it."

"I guess." Ellis checked his watch. "Man, I have to blow on outta here.

Maybeline doesn't feel like working now. And I'm having a couple retired cops handling my other cases and jobs."

Ellis started in the direction of the door.

On the way to his car in the office parking lot, Ellis had to stop and answer his beeper. When he got inside his car he called his office on his cellular phone.

"Mason Detective Agency," the temp secretary said.

"It's me. I got the beep. What's up?"

"You have a message from the mother of Zeke Wilson. She said you should talk to a friend of a woman named Donna. She said the woman. A Betty Williams used to hang around with gang bangers and drug dealers. And she might know where her son is."

"Good. Let me have the address and I'll run by there."

Ellis left his car and entered the yard of a two apartment house on East 58th Street. He climbed the stairs to an outdoor porch and rang the doorbell.

A petite black woman in her twenties with keen-faced features appeared at the screen door.

"Yeah."

"Good morning. I'm Mr. Ellis. I'm looking for a cousin of mine. Zeke Wilson. I can't find him. Somebody told me you could help me locate him."

"Well they told you wrong. I ain't seen Zeke in over five months. And I don't exactly miss him either."

"I know this lady he used to hang with. Her name is Donna Beck."

"Donna. Don't you know? Donna is dead. Somebody killed her."

"Aw man. I don't believe it. Donna. What happened?"

"Her crazy-assed boy friend killed her. At least they arrested him for doing it."

Ellis shook his head. "I'm stunned. I wonder why the guy would do something like that."

"I don't know," Betty said. "It probably wouldn't take much. He was kind of a gangster dude. He had done time before."

"Oh. I wonder did he drag her into the gangster life."

"I really don't know."

"You were friends, weren't you?"

"Yeah. But not that close. She didn't tell me everything."

"Oh. Okay. Thanks for your time. I'll have to find him some other way."

Chapter 13

The car was parked across the street from an apartment building located on the Northwest side of the lake. Inside sat Mel Robinson, a fifty-seven year-old retired cop. Resting on the dashboard was a black and white photograph of Andrea the Mason agency had acquired. On the front seat next to him was a walkie-talkie.

A cab pulled up in front of the building. Andrea emerged from the building carrying a briefcase and a large purse with a shoulder strap. She entered the cab and it drove away.

Robinson spoke into the walkie-talkie. "Miss thing just left for a hard day's work."

"Cool. We'll be on our way in a minute," Ellis said via a walkie-talkie.

Ellis was in a black van parked a block and a half from Andrea's building. In the front seat with him was Chuckie Smith, a dark-skinned young black man that looked like Wesley Snipes goofier brother. Both men wore dark green baseball caps and matching work coveralls.

Ellis turned the key in the van's ignition. "Let's roll."

"Let's rock. Let's rock and roll."

Ellis made the short drive to Andrea's building. He parked out front. Ellis left the van with a long metal toolbox. Chuckie took a clipboard with him. They first moved to the rear of the van.

"Let's get this bad boy on the road," Chuckie said eagerly. "It'll be like old times. Doing a little B&E."

"It won't be like no damn old times. I'm not taking anything. Plus you won't be entering."

Ellis used his key to unlock the van's rear door. He grabbed hold of a five-foot metal ladder.

"I'll take the ladder. You take the board and tools."

"Gotcha."

Ellis knew Andrea's building worked on the dusk to dawn outer door key system. Plus a security guard was on duty at the front entrance. During the day there was open access to the building.

Ellis and Chuckie went through the service entrance and rode the freight elevator to Andrea's floor. They came around a corner and moved to the far end of the hall. Ellis glanced periodically at the light fixture above them that was part of his plan.

"This is it here. We've got the one right nearby."

Ellis set up his ladder underneath a light fixture. He removed a screwdriver from the toolbox.

"Now it's time for the master to go to work," Chuckie proclaimed.

Chuckie moved over and examined the lock on Andrea's door.

"This might be too easy, I think I have a pass key for this one."

Up ahead of the pair, a door to an apartment swung open.

"People," Ellis whispered.

Ellis climbed the ladder and started to unscrew the light fixture covering. Chuckie whirled about and put his back to the door. He went to the toolbox and rummaged about in it. An elderly couple passed them without giving them a second look. Ellis and Chuckie stayed in character until the couple disappeared around the corner. Ellis climbed down the ladder. Chuckie rushed back to the door. From his coverall pocket he took a ring of keys. He picked out a key and tried it in the lock. The door came open.

"I'm bad. I know I'm bad. I'm really bad. Right?"

"Right."

Ellis stepped to the door and handed the screwdriver to Chuckie.

"Aw man. You should let me come in with you."

"I don't think so. Stay here. And try to act like you know what you're doing."

Ellis entered Andrea's apartment and closed the door behind him. He was surprised by the lack of a feminine touch. The furnishings were sparse and stark, the décor a neutral mixture of blacks, whites, and grays.

Ellis searched around the coffee table where the phone rested. Then he noticed an address book has fallen to the carpet. He thumbed through the book, checking the Fs and Ds, not finding Francine's name listed. He went through the special numbers section, getting the same result. He returned the book to the exact same spot on the floor.

Ellis moved to the hall with a bedroom on either side. He eased into the room to his right. It had more of a woman's touch to it. What caught his eye was a pair of poster sized photographs of Andrea. She was nude in both. A rearview of her seated backwards in a wooden chair. A front view of her, one hand covering her crotch, the other over a breast, her lips pouted seductively.

He approached the antique looking dresser. The top drawer was filled with cosmetics and assorted junk. The middle drawer was lined with lingerie. He hit the jackpot in the left-hand corner. Inside a 6x9 envelope were several bank books. Most were from several local branches. The balance in all was no more than four thousand dollars. Among these was a quarterly report from a Swiss bank account. The balance was eighty-five thousand dollars and loose change.

Ellis returned the books to the envelope. From his coverall pocket he took the same type of mini-camera Royce had used before. He used it to photograph the report. The report went back into the envelope. The envelope was returned to the dresser drawer.

Ellis scanned the room. Nothing significant was uncovered.

When he moved to the second bedroom he found that it had been converted to a home office. It was equipped with the typical desk, chairs, table, books, computer, phone, and fax machine.

Ellis approached the desk and tried four drawers to the right and left. The middle drawer was unlocked. To the left he made another discovery. A long business envelope with the hand written initials F.D in the lower left corner. The contents of the envelope was a private investigator's surveillance report. The subject was Francine Darden. The dates of the long report began in late March of 1988 and ended on April 10th of 1988.

Also in the envelope were surveillance photographs. The most interesting featured Francine in various locations with an unidentified man. And of course, Congressman Ryan. In most of the photographs Ryan was wearing dark glasses and some sort of hat. The exception being at political events and at a college baseball game where someone was sitting between him and Francine.

Ellis took photographs of the surveillance pictures and report.

As he left the office he caught a glimpse of movement across the hall in the bedroom. Ellis stepped in and saw Chuckie rummaging through Andrea's lingerie drawer.

"What the hell are you doing?"

Chuckie bolted forward, and then whirled about. "Damn, man. You scared the shit outta me."

"I thought I told you not to come in here."

"I was uh, I was just trying to help out. I guess you saw the bank books."

"Screw that. Turn your pockets inside out."

"Aw man."

"Do it."

"Brother man. How can you humiliate me like this?"

"Just do it."

Chuckie turned all his pockets inside out. "Nothing. I hope you're satisfied."

"Put everything back the way it was so we can get the hell on outta here."

"Yes sir boss. I'm gonna sho do that."

Chuckie started returning items. "You know something, my brother. I think you've got a dangerous babe here. She's got the fly crib, the Swiss bank account. But she has pictures of herself buck naked hanging on the wall. That's some combination." He held up a pair of satin panties. "The last piece." He took a whiff of the panties. "The sweetest smell in the world."

"You're one sick puppy."

"Ain't I though."

Ellis was on his way inside Royce Investigations' office building just as Royce was coming out.

"Hey. I was just coming by hoping you would be here."

"I'm on my way to work on a missing person case."

"You must be into working the field. I mean your family owns the company. You could lay back and push pencils."

"Not my style, babe."

Royce started moving across the parking lot in the direction of a car.

"You're into the Bogart private eye thing, ain't you?"

"A little bit."

"You're not wearing the trench coat."

"I have to do a little updating. If Bogart was around today he'd be more like Al Pacino."

"I could see him in the Godfather movies. But I don't know about the classic Scarface."

They reached a light green Buick.

"So why did you come here this time?" Royce asked.

"I picked up some interesting info on your friend Miss Newsome."

"Yeah. Where did you get it from?"

"I'd rather not say. But I took a page from your book."

"By the time you're finished, I won't have a book left."

"Maybe not. But Miss Newsome has a little bit of money in bank accounts here. She also has eighty plus K in a Swiss bank account. Strange huh?"

"Not particularly. S&L's and banks are having their problems in some places. She's probably just being safe with her money."

"Maybe. I also know she has a P.I's surveillance report on Francine Darden. Done in March and April by another agency. So why didn't she tell you guys she knew about Francine?"

"I don't know. I'm sure she had her reasons."

"I like to hear 'em."

"What are you going to do?"

"Talk to her. And ask her about it."

"I can get us a meeting quicker than you would."

"As long as you don't cramp my style."

"I wouldn't want to do that," Royce said with a smile. "I have to do this. Later we may be able to catch her at home. I'll ring you."

"Cool."

Andrea was at her desk in her home office working on a speech with a pad and pencil when the phone rang. She answered it.

"Hello. I'm busy right now."

"Too busy to talk to a new friend?"

"Is that you, Brad?"

"I'm surprised you know my voice."

"I'm good with voices. What can I do for you?"

"I have something I want to run by and talk to you about. It won't take long."

"Sure. Come on over."

"Okay. I'll be there in about a hour."

"All right. See you then."

Andrea hung up the phone. She was beginning to wonder what Royce wanted when she glanced at the clock on her desk and saw the time. She was about to miss something important on television.

Andrea hurried into her living room. She sat on the sofa and used the remote to snap on the TV. On screen, Ryan was on a news broadcast being interviewed by a female reporter.

"Congressman Ryan," the reporter said. "In view of recent polls that show your Republican opponent closing the gap, are you feeling the heat about how you've conducted your campaign up to now."

"Certainly not. I feel I have a good voting record. I've sponsored legislation to help the region. I'm a good family man that believes in family values. And if I'm elected I won't stop until I've made life better for each and every American."

Knowing what she knew, Ryan's words seemed hilariously funny to Andrea. She started laughing and couldn't contain herself. She slid off the sofa onto the floor and repeatedly banged her fist into the carpet.

Chapter 14

Royce and Ellis were driving in Royce's personal car, a 1988 Mustang. They were on their way to Andrea's. At a traffic light Royce punched on the radio. A reporter on an all news station was saying:

"As George Bush and Michael Dukakis move toward their party's nominations, the conventions now loom ahead. Now the-"

Royce switched the station to a soft rock format.

"What's the matter?" Ellis asked. "You don't care about the future of your country."

"I care." The light changed. Royce hit the gas petal. "I care. I'm just tired of hearing the same old story all day."

"Me, myself, I hope Bush don't get in there."

"Yeah. Why not?"

"Reagan kicked me in the butt bad enough. Bush'll be a goofy acting version of Reagan."

"I'll take Bush over the lovely and dull Dukakis."

"Let's face it, neither one 'em is ever gonna be added to Mt. Rushmore."

"I hear you."

Andrea moved across her living room to answer the door. She had changed from a blouse and jeans to a hot pink shirt-dress that stopped four inches above her knee. She knew dressing somewhat provocatively would divert a man's attention even if she wasn't his type.

Andrea partially cracked the door open. "Hi there."

"Hello. You're looking great as always," Royce said.

"You're too nice."

Andrea opened the door further and Ellis came into view.

"Hello. I'm Ellis Mason."

"Oh. Nice to meet you."

They shook hands.

"Same here."

"Ellis is an associate of mine."

"Come on in."

Andrea led the way. She sat on the sofa. Royce joined her. Ellis sat in an easy chair opposite them.

A bottle of red wine in a container of crushed ice rested on the clear glass table in front of the sofa.

"Red wine, gentlemen."

"None for me," Ellis said.

"I'll have some."

Andrea poured two glasses of wine. She handed one to Royce and kept the other. She crossed her legs and slipped from her glass.

"So what's the important matter you want to discuss?"

"It has to do with the work we did for you and Cody," Royce said. "Especially regarding Francine Darden."

"That's over with, isn't it? I mean the poor child was murdered. We can't even use the info we have on the affair with Ryan. If the police are smart they may make the connection and expose it for us, which of course, would be the best thing."

"We think Francine may have been involved with something illegal," Ellis said. "It may have gotten her killed."

"Oh yes." Andrea took another swig from her wine. "I recall Brad mentioning some such thing. I can't imagine how you think I could be of help to you."

"Miss Darden had your phone number in her address book. Have you ever had any contact with her?"

"None whatsoever. Unless I spoke with her briefly at a public function."

"Do you have any idea why she had your phone number?"

Andrea uncrossed her legs. "To ask for help in finding a job? I really couldn't say."

Royce gulped down the remainder of his drink and stood. "Well. We don't want to take up any more of your time. Thanks for the help."

"Any time. Nice to meet you Mr. Ellis."

"Yeah."

Ellis wasn't really in the mood to leave, but couldn't see how he could get out of going along with Royce.

Out in the hall, after Andrea had shut the door, Ellis fed Royce a knowing glance.

"Don't say it. Just don't say it."

Andrea crossed the room and returned to the sofa area. She half filled a glass with wine and drank it with one gulp. She refilled the glass to the top.

Pacing about, Andrea wondered how and why her luck had suddenly turned so rotten. If a couple incidents had come about differently she would be looking at smooth sailing to her goal. Now she was wading through knee deep murky water. She had an idea of how she would handle Royce. She knew Ellis would be a harder nut to crack. She had sensed he was skeptical of her explanations. Maybe he even knew more than he was letting on. He would have to be diverted, placated, or eliminated.

Andrea finished off her drink and weighed if she should have another.

Benny walked along the hall, gazing all around him to see if any one was watching. He stopped outside Francine's apartment and used the key he had to get inside. The place looked lifeless and abandoned. Things were ajar. Not where Francine would've had them. He knew the cops had gone all over the place after the murder. He was just hoping against hope they had left something behind that tied him to Francine. He would scoop it up and destroy it.

Benny began looking for an address book around the phone. Gone. He looked for anything around the bookcase. Nothing. He went to the bedroom and cut through things there. Not a thing. Not a damn thing. He was desperate enough to try the kitchen, the toilet top in the bathroom. Forget it, he finally thought.

Benny was beginning to see only one way out. Haul ass out of town.

A four-wheel drive enclosed jeep drove up and parked in front of a neighborhood pool hall.

Getting out on the driver's side was Mongo Pike, a stocky beer bellied man with long sandy hair, an unruly beard, and a hook-like nose. He was wearing baggy pants and a white T-shirt with the words KISS MY ASS across it in black letters.

Zeke Wilson left the passenger's side. He was six-three and muscular with ruggedly handsome features. He had a medium brownskinned complexion and wore his hair in the Larry Blackmon Cameo style.

Mongo and Wilson headed in the direction of the pool hall.

"You know this ain't gonna be nothing but bull shit, don't you?" Mongo asked.

"Not necessarily."

"Bull shit."

"You wouldn't be saying that if it was about you."

There were eight pool tables in the typically dark and smoke filled poolroom. Most of the patrons were black or Hispanic men.

Wilson and Mongo walked in. Wilson scanned the room and found what he was looking for. He started in the direction of a Coke machine along the wall.

Standing next to the Coke machine was a smallish black guy wearing a backwards bright orange beret, red shirt, and burgundy pants. They called him Bobo.

"My brother."

"Bobo."

They gave each other a soul handshake.

"What have you got for me?" Wilson asked.

"Where's the juice? I need that juice bad."

Maybe you need it too damn much." Wilson reached into his pocket and removed a ten-dollar bill. "Tell me something good."

"This bitch I know, she tells me some brother was passing himself off as your cousin. And he was trying to find you."

"Cousin. What the fuck did he look like?"

"Average size. A little over thirty."

"I don't know no damn body like that. Not nobody that don't know where I'm at. Or would try to track me. Did he seem like Five-O?"

"Not from what the bitch said, Ier, I been hearing that boy Armad has people trying to get him out from under being busted for whacking

Donna."

"Yeah. I'll tell you what. Work that Armad thing for me. I want a name on his people."

Wilson gave Bobo another fifteen dollars.

"You got it babe. I'll be working it like a dog."

Ellis sat nursing a drink at the type of hot, funky, sticky inner-city bar he never frequented unless it was work related. The music was ear splitting, the cheap wine and beer flowing with ease. At almost any time verbal and physical altercations could erupt.

The mood of the bar fit his mind-set. The interrogation of Andrea proved she was lying, and obviously hiding something. He had no idea what, or how to go about finding out.

Time was moving on from the date of J.C's murder. All he had was disconnected bits and pieces that may never come together and fit. He felt like he was swimming in a sea of sharks just waiting to devour him and make him disappear forever. What he really needed was a break that might not come to fruition in a timely manner.

Chapter 15

It was the early afternoon of the following day. Royce was lying out in his bed with stereo headphones covering his ears. The phone rang as he was listening Freddy Jackson's Nice N' Slow. Royce removed the headphones and lifted the receiver.

"Hello."

"Hi there. Do you know who I am?"

"Sure do. Andrea. What's up?"

"I've been thinking about you lately. I know it's on short notice. But would you like to have dinner with me this evening?"

"Dinner. Yeah. Sure. What do you like? Where would you like to go?"

"I know a great Mexican place downtown."

The Mexican restaurant was spacious and divided into booths. The artwork, plants, and decorations had a south of the border feel to them. The waiters and waitresses wore nineteenth century style Mexican aristocrat costumes.

Royce and Andrea sat side by side in their booth, he in a gold Armani, she in a low cut white wrap around dress. They hand an entrée of tacos washed down with tequila.

"I have a question for you, Mr. Man," Andrea said. "How did you become a shamus, a P.I, a private dick? How, how, how? Don't tell me. You're a bitter ex-cop unjustly booted from the force."

"You have it down. You nailed me. I'm going to nail those bastards and collect my pension," Royce said with conviction.

"Really. Is that true?"

"Gotcha. Actually, my father started the business over twenty years ago. It must be in the family's blood. I like the business. I like taking part in it. How did you become an ace political consultant?"

Andrea sipped from her tequila. "It's nothing too dramatic or interesting. I was just a little smart kid that made straight A's. Actually, I was pretty fat until I got to high school. You may not believe it, but I'm all for order and stability in my life. In 1968, at the height of bleeding heart liberalism, I decided to become a Young Republican. When Abbie Hoffman and all those clowns were disrupting the Democratic convention, I was hanging on Nixon's every word when he talked about law and order. Of course, he disappointed me with the Watergate thing. So did Ford. But Ronald Reagan, oh my God. I just love him. I think he's great. If he was twenty or thirty years younger, I would just stalk him and track him down, and just screw his brains out."

Royce smiled and chuckled. "Why does he have to be so much younger?"

"Well darling. I wouldn't want to kill the man."

"Are you that great?" Royce asked with amusement.

Andrea smiled. "Well, that would be a matter of opinion."

"I read in an article that sex appeal has to do with a person's personal confidence and self image."

"Interesting." Andrea took a bite out of her taco. "How is your self image?"

"Not bad. It could be better. I've had my share of broken romances. What about your's?"

"It's great right about now. Sexually and professionally. I feel like I've reached my era. I think this is the time for the killer elite."

"Killer elite?"

"I'm just talking about the best having a chance to be the best. The smartest, the most prepared, the hardest working getting the spoils of victory."

"And what might those spoils be?"

Andrea fed him her short, quick smile. "Why Mr. Man. Money, of course. I love money. Is there anything wrong with that?"

"No."

Andrea and Royce moved up the walk toward her building.

"It's a nice cool night, isn't it?" Andrea asked.

"Yeah. They're saying it might really get hot this summer."

They reached the front entrance. "I got you here safely. I guess you can take it from here."

"I don't know. This building is more dangerous than you think."

"Then I must escort you to your door."

"Then you must come in for one last drink."

"If I must I must."

Andrea entered the apartment first. She snapped on the switch along the wall. A dim ceiling bulb lit the room. Royce followed her inside.

"What are you drinking? I have some great brandy in the frig."

"Sounds good to me."

"Two brandies coming up."

Andrea headed out of the room.

Royce sat on the sofa in a state of confusion. He had no idea where the evening with Andrea was going. Since the AIDS scare had come to the forefront he had lost what little touch he had in the seduction of the opposite sex.

Andrea returned carrying a tray that contained a bottle of brandy and two glasses. She sat down next to Royce and poured the drinks. They drank in silence for several moments.

"You're suddenly very quiet," Andrea said.

"Yeah. I'm not too good at this. I mean, I really don't know what this is. I've had a bad time with women lately."

"Welcome to the club. I haven't been to lucky with men lately."

Royce drank from his brandy. "I don't know if I can believe that."

"I suppose I've been too career conscious in recent years. But I think I'm ready to change that............You know what I think we should do?"

"What?"

Just get the sex thing out of the way first. And then just go from there."

"Oh. Good idea. But I didn't, you know, come prepared."

"I don't want you to get the wrong idea. But." Andrea reached for a decorative jar on the coffee table. She lifted the top. Inside were several condoms. "I haven't used these in several weeks. Trust me."

Before Royce had time to react Andrea laced him with quick kisses to the neck and cheek. To him each kiss was like being jabbed with a branding iron. She then planted a shock wave jolt directly on his lips. They double-tongued each other on the second and third long, hot, burning kiss.

Royce was completely wrapped up and taken. "Your tits. I want 'em."

Andrea unsnapped her wrap around dress. She slid her arms out of the dress and let it tumble to her waist. Royce kissed her neck, went straight downward, and slid over to her left breast, then the right. He ran his tongue around the area of her nipples.

"This is so great," Andrea moaned. "Come eat me baby. Come eat me."

Andrea stood on the sofa seat. She let her dress fall to her ankles. She stepped out of her panties one leg at a time.

Royce began at her belly button and moved down to her honey pot. He ate her out slowly, getting the taste of sour strawberries.

"Oh baby baby. Baby, baby," purred Andrea.

Royce grabbed hold of her tight buns, inserting one finger. He increased the pace. Her juices began to flow. She cried out in orgasm.

Andrea stepped down off the sofa, picked out a spot on the carpet, and lay on her back.

"Come do me right now. Please. Hurry up. Hurry."

Royce came to his feet. He quickly tossed away his shoes and coat. He unfastened his pants and climbed out of them. A condom was taken from the jar. Once the raincoat was in place, he pounced upon Andrea, entering her immediately. All his penned up feelings about women seemed to spur him on. He plowed into her at a continuously frenetic pace.

Andrea twisted her head from side to side, clutched the carpet, and kicked her legs high in the air. "Yes, yes. Oh yes, yes, yes!"

Royce shot his wad and tingled all over.

"Please get up now," Andrea ordered.

"Why? What for?"

"Just get off."

Royce backed away and rose to his knees. Andrea slid from under him and came to her feet. She suddenly was playful again.

"Last one to the bedroom is a rotten egg."

She dashed off ahead of Royce. His effort to get up and go caused him to slip on the carpet and bang his knee into an easy chair.

"Ouch. Damn. Ouch."

When he reached the bedroom Andrea was already in bed. Her back rested against the headboard, her legs spread completely apart.

"Are you still hungry?" she asked seductively. "Come get some more to eat."

"Yes ma'am. Here I come."

Royce hit the bed on all fours and crawled toward his target. This time he used his tongue to work Andrea into frenzy. Royce found himself floating through a super high state of consciousness. One second he was going down on Andrea. The next she was seated straddle him riding his rod like a freaked out bucking bronco. And then he was drifting off to sleep with Andrea's head buried into his chest.

The following morning, wearing only an oversized blouse, Andrea stood at the stove cooking scrambled eggs and bacon. Royce half stumbled into the room in just his shoes and pants.

"Hey."

"Good morning. You're witnessing a rare sight. Me cooking breakfast for a man. Me cooking breakfast for me is a pretty rare also. There's some milk and juice in the frig."

Royce sat at the table. "About last night."

"You don't have to thank me," Andrea said with a smile. "I had fun too."

"So. If I call you, will you go out with me and not put me off?"

"I'll go out with you, and won't put you off."

Chapter 16

Russo was at his desk in the homicide workroom when the call came in. He answered the ringing phone.

"Russo. Homicide."

"Yeah. Are you the one in charge of the Francine Darden case?"

"You got it."

"I have something for you. I can give you the guy who did it."

"I'm listening."

"I can give you where he lives. You might pick up some evidence that'll make the case for you."

"Wait a minute now. What you're telling me. Why should I believe you?"

"I'm calling from a booth. You can't track me. Look. The guy's name is Sammy Hendrics. I'll give you the address and you can do what you want."

Russo and Boulware entered the vestibule of the aging three-story apartment building. Mail slots with names and apartment numbers above them were along the wall to their left. Boulware drifted over and checked the listings.

"Sammy Hendrics. Apartment 310."

"Jesus Christ! The third floor," Russo complained. "Three goddamned flights of stairs. I'm starting to feel older than this dump looks."

"Clean living will save you, my man."

"It's too fucking late for that now."

Boulware and Russo made the three flight trek. Boulware opened a lead and maintained it all the way up to 310. He knocked and waited. Knocked and waited. Knocked and waited.

"He's either gone or isn't answering. I guess we better check with the manager. A sign was on the ground floor."

"Shit. Here I go again."

They returned to the first floor and knocked until a balding gray-haired man with age spots dotting his face cracked the door open.

"Yeah. What can I do for you?"

Boulware flashed his badge. "We're looking for Sammy Hendrics.

Nobody answered his door."

"He should be up there. What's the problem? Did the kid do something wrong? I couldn't imagine that he would."

"Why do you say that?" Russo asked.

"Well, the kid is, uh, special, you know. A little slow in the thinking department. But he has a good heart. He'll give you the shirt off his back. He works at a mailroom at a company not too far from here. The kid does okay. But he just doesn't understand some things."

"You may be right," Boulware said. "We have a complaint on him. You could help us out if you can get us in his apartment so we can look around."

"I don't... I don't know if I should do that. Don't you need a warrant?"

"Not if you give us permission."

"I'm not sure I should."

"Look, you said he may be at home. Maybe something's wrong. We can check it out."

"All right. I'll go get a key."

The door to Sammy's apartment swung open. There was a narrow hall running straight ahead with rooms to the left and at the end, to the right.

Boulware and Russo walked in and stepped into the first room on the left.

"Aw, man."

"Unbelievable."

The room was a photographic shrine to Francine Darden. There were photographs of her walking the street, seated at an outdoor café, getting in and out of cars, on the beach in a series of bathing suits, head shots of her with a variety of facial expressions. The photographs, some blown up to various sizes, were plastered over every inch of the room's walls.

The only furnishings in the room were a wide-screen television set, a couple overstuffed chairs, and a cassette storage rack.

Russo and Boulware moved around the room, scanning the photographs along the walls.

"This is classic stuff," Boulware said. "Stalker behavior. Obsessed fan."

"And maybe killer."

There was a grunting sound coming from another room in the apartment, followed by a loud thud. Boulware and Russo drew their guns and raced down the hall. Russo swung into a bedroom first, followed by Boulware.

Sammy Hendrics was sprawled out on the floor near the bed. He was a big man of six-four with a puffy Pillsbury doughboy body. He sat up and gazed at the men who had invaded the room. From his features and movements it was easy to tell he was mentally impaired.

"Hi there. Are those water pistols?"

Russo and Boulware put their weapons away. Russo took out his badge.

"We're police officers."

"I rolled over too far. Fell outta bed," Sammy said.

Sammy struggled to his feet. For a while he wiped his eyes with the back of his hand.

"Aren't you going to ask why we're here?"

"Uh... uh. Are you like the guys on Miami Vice and those other shows?"

"We're here to ask you about Francine Darden," Boulware said.

Sammy shook his head from side to side vigorously. "I don't. I don't. I don't know her."

"Are you sure about that? We saw the pictures on the wall in the other room."

"Pretty girls. Pretty pictures. I like 'em."

"Can we go see them now?"

"Okay. Pretty girls. Pretty girls."

Sammy led the way. Russo and Boulware trailed after him. Along the way Russo threw Boulware a questioning glance.

The trio entered the bedroom.

"That's Francine there. Don't you know her? Russo asked.

"Pretty girls. I used to have another person on the wall. Daryl."

"A guy?"

"The fish lady. The fish movie. She's from here."

"Are you talking about Daryl Hannah, the actress?" Boulware asked.

"Yeah. She was up there. Now I have her."

"Did you take those pictures, Sammy?"

"I have to pee. I have to pee real bad."

Russo stepped forward angrily. "Look, I'm tired of you not answering the question. I don't know what your I.Q. is, but you better start listening up."

Sammy began to bounce up and down like a little kid. "I have to pee. I have to pee. Can I go pee?"

"Yeah, go on," Boulware said.

Sammy turned in the direction of the hall. Russo blocked his path.

"Wait a minute. Let me check the room first."

Russo stepped out ahead and entered the bathroom first. He looked inside the medicine cabinet. Checked the dirty clothes hamper. On a whim he lifted the toilet tank top.

"Bingo. I hit the jackpot."

"What is it?" Boulware asked.

Russo placed the top down in a sideways position. From the toilet tank he removed a plastic Ziploc bag containing a .357 Magnum.

"You know what this reminds you of." Russo directed his attention to Sammy. "Is this your gun?"

"Is that a water pistol?"

"Hell, no, it's not no goddamn water pistol. It's a real gun. It could've been used to kill somebody. Now is it yours?"

"Can I pee now? By myself."

"Let's let him pee."

"Shit."

Russo and Boulware left the bathroom and closed the door behind them.

"Same type of gun Francine Darden was shot with," Russo whispered. "We may have our man."

"Maybe so."

Several seconds passed. Russo banged on the door. "Hey, did you fall in?"

There was a scrambling sound from within the bathroom. Russo pushed the door open. Sammy was at the window trying to lift it.

"What the hell do you think you're doing?"

Russo rushed over and grabbed hold of Sammy. He pulled him back around toward the door.

"You're going in. We have to take you in for questioning."

Sammy whimpered and looked frightened and confused. "Take me where? I didn't do anything wrong. I try not to. I always try not to."

"Just calm down. You'll be all right, okay?"

"Okay, okay."

"Give us the name and we'll tell somebody where you are."

Chapter 17

Ryan paced back and forth across his den. All he was trying to do was write a kicker final paragraph to his speech. He was usually pretty damn good at structuring his speeches in his own words. Since he learned of Francine's death, it seemed as though his brain was operating at only seventy-five percent capacity.

Part of him had been wracked with grief. A grief he couldn't follow through on because he wasn't acquainted with her family, and wasn't sure if they knew anything about him.

The rest of him was feeling like the Coyote in the Road Runner cartoons. He was wary of the giant anvil of disclosure crashing down upon his head and smashing him into the turf.

It was too much. Just too damn much.

Ryan glanced at the clock on his desk and saw that the six o'clock news would just be beginning. He snapped on the portable TV in the room. A dark-haired beauty on Channel Seven was saying, "Police have a lead in the drive-by shooting death of Francine Darden. A twenty-seven year old Chicago man, Sammy Hendrics, is being held in connection with the slaying. Police say the murder weapon has been recovered. Formal charges have yet to be filed against Hendrics. In other news..."

Ryan snapped the set off. He breathed a deep sigh of relief. Maybe he had survived. Maybe he was off the hook. He hoped it was so. He promised himself he would stay away from all women other than his wife. And if he ever got extra horny he would just grab a Playboy and beat his meat.

Cody heard the same newscast while seated with his campaign manager, John Brooks.

"They've finally gotten a break in that poor girl's murder," Cody said.

"Hell, it might be a break for us. If it sticks with this guy they've arrested, then the case will be nice and closed. The story will be in the news. Who knows, it may leak out that the dearly departed Miss Darden was a close personal friend of our friend, Congressman Ryan. Good idea or what? Brooks asked.

"Not bad, not bad. If we pick the right time. And, of course, if they can't trace it back to us."

"No problem. I'm a slick and slinky guy."

Later in the evening, Ellis viewed a newscast that delivered the arrest announcement regarding Francine's case. Boulware had briefly appeared on camera saying, "We have reason to believe the suspect may have been stalking the victim for some time before the actual shooting occurred."

All Ellis could think of was his theory of a connection between the murders could be ruined if they had arrested the right man for Francine's murder. J.C.'s murder would be thrown into a gray area, especially if Armad was responsible for Donna's death.

It dawned on him how far he had strayed from his initial intention to clear Armad of the charges against him. He vowed to get back on that angle. Still, he knew he had to get in contact with Boulware. He had to get a clue about what was actually going down.

"Yes! Yes! Oh yes, oh yes. This is... this is so great," moaned Andrea.

Naked, she was on all fours in the middle of the bed. Royce was doing her doggy style at an ever increasing pace. Andrea's sighs and grunts spurred him on to be even more frantic. At their height of passion they had the bed bucking like Linda Blair's in The Exorcist. Royce shot his wad in a continuous flow, threatening to overrun the condom he wore. Royce leaned back and took Andrea with him. It took several moments for them to rev down to normalcy. She pulled away from him and flopped down on her back.

"Oh. Wow, that was so great." Andrea made a deep sigh. "I guess you heard about the arrest in the Francine Darden case."

"Yeah. It looks like she was being stalked by a crazy."

"Do you think your associate, Mr. Ellis, will be satisfied now that the case is closed?"

"I suppose so. At least regarding Miss Darden. He's still going to be looking for whoever killed his partner. I suppose you can't fault him for that. It's a noble thing to do."

"Certainly. I would appreciate it, though, if you would steer him away from me."

"Yeah. But what's in it for me?"

"How much cash do you want?"

"Haven't you heard, darling? The best things in life are free."

"They are, huh. Namely what?"

"Lots of things. Like, uh, blow jobs."

Andrea smiled. "I'm your love slave. I'll do whatever you say."

She tossed away Royce's condom and began stroking him to an erection.

Chapter 18

Ellis was dressed and ready to go when the phone in the living room rang. Part of him wanted to keep going, but not wanting to miss anything important, he moved over and lifted the receiver.

"Yeah. You got me."

"Finally," Zöe said. "I've been calling you and missing you all week. Didn't you get my messages on your machine?"

"Oh. That damn thing ain't been working right. I just haven't had time to get it fixed."

"I've got you now. You want to come by for dinner tonight?"

"I wish I could. But I might have to work. Either on, you know, the J.C. thing. Or some other work. I'm sorry."

"No, you're not. It's just your way of dumping me, isn't it?"

"No. I don't have time to stand here and argue like this."

"Don't hang up on me, you son of a-"

Ellis put the receiver back in place. In a way, he agreed with Zöe. His life recently had been centered around finding a solution to J.C.'s murder. Cracking the case was the only way he wanted to end the work overload.

Ellis' Volvo was parked in the lot of a fast food restaurant. He, however, was across the lot in the front seat of Boulware's car. Both had just picked up potentially fattening orders. A burger, double order of fries, and a milk shake for Boulware. Two cheeseburgers and a Pepsi for Ellis.

"It's put up time, my brother," Boulware said. "You said you were going to give me something you've been holding back on."

"I can. But then I can't."

"Hey, you about to take my patience to the limit."

"Okay. Okay. What I'm saying is if I give up what I've got, it could cause a chain reaction that would blow the thing up in public."

"You make it sound like a world beating situation."

Ellis drank from his Pepsi. "Not world beating. Just Chicago beating."

"I'm still not reading you."

"What's the real reason Chicago is known for being the windy city?"

"Politicians talking loud and saying nothing. Are you saying these murders may be tied to politics in some way?"

"You got it, my man. That's why I'm holding off. If this thing hits the public it might drive the players underground and we'll never get to them."

Boulware took a bite out of his burger. "I hope you're not playing me."

"I'm not... So, how is the case against this Hendrics guy? Is it as good as it sounded on TV?"

"In some ways, yeah. We recovered the murder weapon from his apartment. It had just his prints on it. There were all kinds of pictures of Francine Darden in his apartment. That fits the obsessed stalker profile. But the thing is, this Hendrics guy is mentally retarded."

"What? Ain't it something wrong with that?" Ellis asked. "Stalkers are sick puppies, but they're usually pretty smart. Is he capable of stalking somebody and killing them in a drive-by? Taking the photographs, or even knowing how to drive?"

"We don't know yet. We tried questioning him. But he would either ramble on, or completely clam up. His folks showed up with a lawyer and he advised him not to talk."

"You're gonna have to do a psychological examination on him, aren't you?"

"Yeah. If we end up formally charging him."

Ellis took a long swig from his drink. "I don't know, man. This Hendrics as the killer thing looks like a set-up to me. But I know you guys believe in the KISS system. Keep it simple, stupid. You've got the stalking angle. The gun with the prints on it. So you're going with Hendrics if he's your man or not."

Boulware chuckled. "Come on, man. You don't want Hendrics to be the man. It wrecks your theory that the murders are connected."

"I still say it's a damn good theory."

"How about this? Your client took down his ex. Hendrics was after Miss Darden. He spots your partner and takes him out of the way. A disturbance happens and he has to pass up going after her. So he comes back later and nails her in the drive-by. How does it grab you?"

"Not too tight. It's possible, but I don't buy it."

Ellis found himself on his way to Royce's office yet again. He wondered if he was depending on him too much. It would be a natural tendency. He ran a small semi-struggling agency with a minimum amount of resources. His was a top-notch state-of-the-art operation with almost unlimited resources at their disposal. It was more than superior facilities that kept drawing him back. It was the feeling that if he was to solve the case Royce would somehow play a key role.

"I knew you would call and show up when I heard about the arrest," Royce said as Ellis walked into his office. "I had a feeling the killings weren't related."

Ellis walked over and sat across from Royce at the desk.

"I'm disappointed in you, man. How are you ever going to be the Bogart of the eighties if you keep thinking like the damn cops? You're suppose to think like the much smarter P.I."

"Like you, huh?"

"Exactly like me. I smell a set-up with this Hendrics guy. I found out from a cop that he's mentally challenged. He's not a stalker. He's a patsy."

"Yeah. Who's using him as a patsy?"

"The real killers."

"The real killers. What did they do? Have him on stand-by retainer?"

"Maybe. I don't know. I'll have to keep investigating."

Royce leaned back in his chair. "I think you've been reading too many conspiracy theory books. I bet you think Hendrics was the second gunman in the grassy knoll. At least I hope you're convinced that Andrea is not involved."

"Oh, so now it's Andrea," Ellis said with a smirk. "Are you doing the nasty with the girl? I saw how you was looking at her. I thought she was digging you back."

"Not that it's any of your business, but we have begun a relationship."

"I hope you know what you're getting yourself into."

"I think I do. And I think I like it a whole lot."

Chapter 19

Ellis was at the desk in his office trying to catch up on the backlog of paperwork from other cases and jobs. Since he had returned from Royce's office he had been in a sluggish mood. He was fighting the urge to put his head on the desk and take a nap, like he used to in school.

The phone on the desk sounded off. He answered it.

"Mason Detective Agency."

"Yeah, uh... are you the man that's been looking for Zeke Wilson?"

"That's me. Do you know where I can find him?"

"I don't," a young black woman said. "But I have a lady friend that do know."

"Can you get her to come down and speak with me?"

"She won't do it. But she will come to my place if you want to talk to her there."

"Uh, can I have your name and address?"

"I'm Carol Johnson. I live at 345 West 48th Street."

Ellis wrote the address down on a pad. "When would be the best time for me to come?"

"Right now. You better hurry up. She may change her mind and take off."

"Okay. I'll be there."

"All right. See you then."

Ellis was so hyped up to have a potential lead that he didn't think to check the phone book to see if Carol Johnson lived at the address she gave him.

Ellis came up the stairs of the apartment building hall, which was dimly lit with a low watt bulb that gave off a surrealistic yellowish glow.

The place he sought was only a couple of doors down from the staircase. He got there and knocked. A heavy-set dark-skinned woman cracked the door open.

"Good evening. I'm Ellis Mason. I just talked to you on the phone about a friend that might know where I can find Zeke Wilson."

"Okay. I'm Carol. Come on in."

She opened the door further and backed several steps away from it.

As he stepped inside, Ellis wondered why she backed off so far. Like a football quarterback that doesn't feel a blind-side hit coming, the impact of the blow to the head by an unseen billy club had an even more devastating affect. He was unable to stop himself from crumbling to the floor. Through the pain in his head and the ringing in his ears, he tried to tell himself to stand, but the message wasn't getting through.

With blurred vision Ellis made out a pair of incongruous figures. A chubby Richard Nixon and a muscular Mickey Mouse. Nixon came over and glared down at him. He couldn't completely make out what he was saying.

"'Ho the 'uck are you? Who t- fuck are 'ou? 'Ho the fuc- 'r- you?"

Nixon went all the way down and lifted Ellis' wallet from his pants pocket.

"He's a 'ucking private 'tective. Son 'f a 'itch!"

Ellis felt the sensation of being lifted. And then flying backwards and crashing into something hard. More pain. But also a jolt that cleared his head somewhat.

Mickey raced toward him. "I don't know who sent you here! Or why the fuck they did, but you in a world of hurt."

Three hard shots to the ribs followed by two more jolts to the stomach. Intense pain followed by a numbness.

"I'm a bad motherfucker, and if you come around me again, your next stop will be six foot under."

Ellis was helpless to prevent the pair of men from dragging him from the room and down the hall to the stairs. And then he was flying through the air, landing with a thud, and rolling, rolling, rolling.

Pain. Pain. And more pain. Pain everywhere, especially in his head and ribs. His head began to swirl. And then he was gone.

Ellis wasn't sure how long he had been out when his eyes popped open. The pain was still there. It was concentrated in his ribs and battered legs from the fall.

Surprisingly, a clear line of thought immediately popped into his head. He had been set up. By their builds and voice tones, one black, one white, the men in the Halloween masks had to be Wilson and Pike. Good news. He was onto something. Bad news. It could get him killed.

Ellis struggled to his feet. With great trepidation he inched his way down the staircase, taking at least four minutes. He stood in the vestibule and took several breaths. He left the building glad that his car was parked only a few strides away. The door on the driver's side was unlocked. He slid inside behind the wheel, fighting through the pain. Being able to drive home seemed out of the question.

Ellis retrieved his cellular phone from the glove compartment. He still had temps manning the office. The two ex-cops he was using were out working other jobs. He reluctantly dialed Royce Investigations. A secretary told him Royce was unavailable. He asked to be put through to Michelle Grant.

"Hello. How may I help you?"

"I'm Ellis Mason. Do you remember me being at your office?"

"Sure. You're a detective."

"Are you busy right now?"

"Not too. Why?"

"I'm, uh, in a little trouble out here in the field. I would need you to take a cab to my location and then drive me home."

"My God. Are you hurt that bad?"

"I'm not in big trouble. Just in some pain."

"Okay. I'll get there as quick as I can. Just give me the address."

While he was waiting for Michelle to arrive, Ellis punched on the car radio. All he got was dance music with a pounding beat or hip hop tunes with a heavy bass line. Where was James Brown doing "I Feel Good" when you needed him?

A cab finally drove onto the scene. Ellis hit the horn and waved. He slid over and let Michelle enter on the driver's side.

"Hi. Are you feeling better?"

"Yeah. It only hurts when I breathe."

"What happened?"

"I had a bad experience with Richard Nixon and Mickey Mouse."

"What?"

"I was set up. And then I got knocked around by two guys. They were wearing Halloween masks. But I would be willing to bet that they were Zeke Wilson and Mongo Pike."

"Oh, my God! What will you do now?"

"Stay on the case. That's all I can do."

Michelle started the car. "Where are we going?"

"To my place."

"Where is it located?"

"South Shore."

"My place is a lot closer. And there's a clinic nearby in case you have to go."

Michelle had a loft type apartment with a living room that led directly into a small kitchen. The chairs and sofas were covered with fringed material done in retro-hippie designs.

Michelle stepped in first. A hobbling, slow moving Ellis trailed her in. They started in the direction of the sofa.

"What do you need?" Michelle asked.

"Some antiseptic for where I got whacked in the head. Do you have any over-the-counter pain tablets?"

"Yeah. I'll be right back."

Michelle moved in the direction of the adjoining bedroom.

Ellis went to the sofa. He had to lean back and ease himself downward.

Michelle returned with a glass of water and a couple capsules on a tray and a bottle of hydrogen peroxide.

"Here it is. I hope it'll help you."

Ellis swallowed the pills. Michelle took a bag of cotton balls from her dress pocket. She soaked a cotton ball in peroxide and dabbed on the spot where Ellis had been clubbed.

"You were hit pretty good. Does this happen to you all the time?"

"Not hardly. Thank goodness. Oh, I need you to help me out a little, if you can. I need a background work-up on Sammy Hendrics, the suspect in the Darden case. He's mentally challenged. He's probably had special schooling and other programs. And Andrea Newsome. She-"

"I know who she is."

"I guess Brad has mentioned her to you."

"Boy has he mentioned her. What has she got to do with all this?"

"I'm not sure yet. But she had a connection with Francine Darden before your agency found out about her affair with Ryan."

"That's wild. Are you sure you feel all right?"

"I'm so tired. I think I'll lie down awhile."

Ellis slept for over twenty minutes. When he awoke, the pain in his head had subsided, but his ribs had stiffened and the sharp throbbing was still there.

He let Michelle drive him to the clinic. An X-ray was done of his ribs. A slight crack was found. He was given a pain-killing shot. He left with his ribs wrapped, armed with medication, and the advice to take it easy a few days, something he couldn't afford to do.

Hand in hand, Royce and Andrea walked slowly near the shore at Oak Street beach. She wore a workout bra and cut-off jeans. Royce had on a pair of khaki summer pants and a tank top.

"You've gone quiet on me again," Andrea said.

"I've been thinking on something. Something I want to tell you. I don't want to scare you off or anything, but I'm really starting to care about you. You know, seriously."

Andrea didn't answer right away. "I've only known you a short time. But I am quite impressed with you."

"Whew! That's a load off my mind."

"Why? Did you think I was going to laugh in your face? You think I'm a cold-blooded love 'em and leave 'em career woman bitch, don't you?"

"No."

"You do, too."

Andrea playfully slapped Royce's chest. She spun away from him and took off running down the beach.

"Come back here, you career girl bitch."

Royce chased after Andrea. As he closed in on her, he reached out and grabbed onto her top at the shoulder. She tried to twist away. Their legs became entangled and they tumbled to the ground. They cracked up laughing.

"I feel good," Andrea said, flashing a larger than usual smile. "I haven't felt this good in a long time."

Chapter 20

Mel Robinson, Chuckie, three black men, a black woman, and two white guys that worked part time for Ellis' agency were assembled in the office, some sitting, some standing. Ellis stood leaning against the front of the desk.

"I want to thank you all for coming on such short notice. On, uh, mostly volunteer operation. You all knew J.C. I think this move will be the best, and maybe the last chance we have of getting the people responsible for his murder. We're going to be focusing on a woman named Andrea Newsome." Ellis removed a photo from a folder on the desk and held it up. "I've prepared an information sheet on her. It may be updated shortly. What we're going to do is put this woman under twenty-four hour surveillance. I've put together a tentative schedule. It could be subject to change. We can all start with our own personal cars. As we go on, I've made arrangements with a car rental company. That's about everything I wanted to cover. Any questions?"

Michelle had halfway blackmailed Ellis into meeting her for lunch at a soul food diner located on the far south side of the downtown area. She wouldn't give him the reports on Andrea and Sammy Hendrics unless he agreed to the date.

The diner was divided into three-sided booths that could hold up to six people. Photographs of well-known Chicago blacks like Harold Washington, John H. Johnson, Ernie Banks, Walter Payton, and Michael Jordan dotted the walls.

Ellis and Michelle sat across from each other at a booth. She was having a weight conscious lunch of vegetable salad and fruit juice. He pigged out on pork chops, fries and a soft drink.

"So, I guess we should get started." Michelle lifted a folder from the booth seat and placed it on the table top. "Here you go."

"Can you give me a run down on what you uncovered?"

"I could. But what's in it for me?"

"What do you want, baby?"

"I'll get to that later." Michelle sipped from her juice. "I have something interesting on your Miss Newsome. When she was in college she was caught up in a cheating scandal. A student romanced a professor. She got hold of a test and farmed it out to other people she knew."

"Was Andrea the romancer?"

"Don't know. It was sort of left hanging. She transferred to another college. Another time, when she was a speech writer, she once borrowed heavily from somebody else's speech without giving them credit. It caused a minor uproar. But the problem was passed off as an oversight in preparing the final text. I guess it proves she's not above crossing the line a little."

"Yeah. This case has three women that could have a little larceny in their hearts. Two are dead. And one is still alive."

Ellis stabbed a piece of pork chop and chewed it. "What did you get on Hendrics?"

"He attended special education schools like you thought he might've. He didn't have a record of any type of violent anti-social behavior. In fact, because of his large size, he was hassled by groups of kids and wouldn't fight back."

"Interesting."

"The only thing resembling any kind of potential stalker type behavior was him getting caught with a girlie magazine in his locker when he was in grade school, and later getting nailed for peeping in the girl's shower room."

"It sounds more like curious kid prank behavior to me." Ellis downed the remainder of his pop. "What is it you want from me?"

"I haven't decided yet. I'm studying you. Searching for the right thing to spring on you."

"I'm scared now," Ellis said with a smile.

Ellis moved through the police workroom until he reached the desk where Boulware was seated.

"My brother Boulware."

"Hey. Have a seat."

Ellis sat down across from Boulware. "Where's Russo? He's not lurking around a corner with a rubber hose waiting to beat information out of me, is he?"

"He's not that bad. He went to grab a bite to eat. Okay, hit me with it. You got that look in your eye."

"I just want to ask you if you checked up on Hendrics' background from school and work."

"Yes, we did. You know we did. You probably have too. And you know he has no history of violence."

"Doesn't that make you have second thoughts?"

"Me, yes. Russo and my captain, not so much. His lawyer is putting heat on us by threatening to go to the press with the story of the cops railroading a retarded kid on a shaky murder charge."

"So what will they do? Will they let him out on bail?"

"Don't know about the bail thing. I hear the state's attorney may put it before the grand jury."

"I guess they have to do something. The case has been out in the press." Ellis leaned back in his seat. "This is your lucky day. I'm going to give you something that'll make you a hero when the case is broken and you nail the right people."

Boulware chuckled. "I can't wait to hear it."

"There's a woman named Andrea Newsome. She works for a political consultant, Marty Silver. You need to check her bank accounts for any recent large withdrawals. You should check her phone records. See if she made or received any phone calls from Francine Darden."

"What reason should I give for having this done?"

"Uh, a private detective. A guy named Rich Spivey. She hired him to follow and report on Francine Darden. That ties her to an open murder case."

"Is there anything more I should know about this woman?"

"No."

Boulware fed Ellis a skeptical glance. "You wouldn't be bullshitting me, would you?"

"Certainly not. If something pops big I'll lay it all in your lap. And you, too, can be a big star."

"If you're finished, get the hell on outta here. Russo may be back soon."

Ellis had picked up his shift of surveillance duty while Andrea was still at work. He had tailed her from work to home. Now, his car was parked across the street from her building. He planned to stay a couple hours, long enough to determine if she planned on going out for the evening.

From his car he saw a group of young men and women in their twenties walk past. They were laughing, talking, and having fun. They were around the same age as J.C. The kids would hopefully go on to lead happy and productive lives. J.C. would never get the chance. Would never move from his twenties into his thirties.

Ellis thought about his very own life. He had been in his twenties mostly during the slap-dash seventies. A decade that seemed to have no particular rhyme or reason. The front end saw the decline in the social impact of the sixties upheaval. Bobby Kennedy and Martin Luther King, Jr. were assassinated. Black revolutionary leaders were dead, in jail, exiled, or on the run. The Viet Nam war ended just in time for the economy to bog down, and our last bit of innocence was dashed by the Watergate scandal. With things crumbling more and more by the minute, we put on blinders, slipped on platform shoes, and danced the night away, mostly to mediocre disco music. The emerging women's movement had one tremendous byproduct for Ellis. Armed with the pill, women were ready and willing to express their liberation sexually. Back in those days, Ellis was able to accommodate them easily.

J.C. had reached his twenties during the Reagan eighties. With their 'rich and white is better than anybody else' attitude, Ellis could see how a young brother like J.C. could be misdirected into criminal behavior, thinking it was his only way out. He thought hiring J.C. would send him down a path to a better life. He never thought J.C. would want to become an operative. He never thought he would become good at it. He never thought it would get him killed.

More than ever, Ellis was determined to solve the case.

Twenty minutes went by. Night set in. Ellis dozed off for a few minutes. He popped awake in time to see a well-dressed man strolling up the walk toward the entrance. He appeared to be carrying a gift wrapped box. Ellis lifted a pair of binoculars off the seat and peered through them.

"Damn, it's my boy, Royce." Ellis grinned. "I don't need three guesses to figure out where he's going. Damn. Buying her gifts already. The boy has his nose open. I just hope he doesn't get it bitten off."

Maybeline had gotten over the paralyzing grief brought on by J.C.'s death. Now she was determined to take an active part in finding his murderer. She hadn't wanted to return to her desk job. She wanted to take part in the team surveillance. Ellis couldn't bring himself to argue her down. However, he did steer her into an early morning shift, hoping she wouldn't have to do too much work.

Maybeline sat in a small Toyota listening to an early morning talk show. She glanced over and saw a red Corvette exit an underground parking lot. She checked a sheet she had on the dashboard. The license plate on the car matched what she had written on the sheet.

Maybeline followed Andrea's car a relatively short distance to an upscale health club. Andrea parked in the lot. Maybeline found a spot on the street.

She had been told to just log in where she went and how long Andrea stayed, but she had a gut feeling she could do more if she handled it right. She left her car and headed for the health club entrance.

Maybeline entered the health club lobby breathing heavily and in a harried state. She bee-lined over to the receptionist.

"Am I too late? Am I too late?"

"Too late for what?" the receptionist asked.

"Andrea Newsome. I was supposed to be her guest. I was supposed to be her guest, but I'm late. I've been running late all day."

"I know the feeling. She just came in. You can catch up with her in the locker room."

"Okay. Thanks."

Maybeline stepped into the club. She was impressed by how nice the place looked. Much better than the community center where she sometimes took exercise classes. She had to ask someone to point her in the direction of the locker room.

Maybeline came in and discovered the typical rows of metal lockers. Instead of tiled or concrete floors there was short-piled wall-to-wall carpet. Extra mirrors lined the walls. Even the benches in front of the lockers were padded.

She reached the rows of lockers just in time to catch a pair of perfect hard bodies strolling in from the shower. Just what I need to see, she thought. Top heavy and big hipped me bearing witness to a pair of ultra babes.

She got back on track. She spotted Andrea in the process of changing from her street clothes to her exercise gear. She moved to the next row and sought what she needed. A woman her basic size and weight. She found her near the end of the row. Maybeline moved in next to her. She searched through her purse.

"Damn! I don't believe it."

"What happened?" the woman asked.

"I went off and forgot my leotard. Are you a member here? Do you have an extra one?"

"Yes, I do. You're welcome to use it."

Maybeline changed into the leotard as quickly as possible. She reached the end of the aisle in time to see Andrea exit the room. She waited a couple beats before following her out. In a slow moving, nonchalant manner, Maybeline followed Andrea down the hall and around a corner to the machine and weight room.

In the room, several men and women of various ages, sizes and shapes worked out on machines, exercise bikes, and with weights.

Andrea was busy on a bicycle. The others next to her were occupied. Maybeline drifted about as if she was trying to decide what she wanted to work on. When one of the people working next to Andrea stopped and moved on, Maybeline quickly slid in next to her.

She had it in her mind that she could stay with Andrea and they would finish pedaling at the same time. Her legs started getting tired and heavy, her heart feeling like it was going to burst from her chest. She breathed a deep sigh of relief when Andrea slowed her pedaling to a stop, allowing her to do the same.

"Whew! Why do we torture ourselves like this?"

"To feel better about ourselves."

"To impress a man."

"To keep a man happy. Sad but true," Andrea said, smiling.

"This exercise stuff is harder than my work."

"Yeah. What do you do?"

"I'm a secretary. For a law firm. What about you?"

"I'm a political consultant. I help run campaigns for politicians."

"Really. Are you working on a campaign right now?"

"James Cody's, yes."

"I've heard of him. He sounds kind of interesting."

"Really. You'd be interested in supporting a Republican candidate?"

"Maybe. You know, I'd have to hear a little more from him."

Andrea dismounted from the bike and stretched her legs. "You could see him in person tonight. There's a fundraiser at the Drake Hotel. I think there's a few tickets left."

"How much will they go for?"

"It's a seventy-five a plate dinner. Plus any contributions you want to make."

"O-o-o-o-h. That's too rich for my monthly budget."

"Oh, there'll be other appearances coming up."

"Good. I'll have to check him out."

After getting the report from Maybeline, Ellis decided he should keep his 'woman as good luck charm' thing going. The females he hired had other things to do. An alternative came to mind. He picked up the phone in his office and dialed a number.

"Hello."

"Hi. It's me."

"Me. Me who?" Michelle asked.

"You know what me. It's the Ellis me."

"Oh, that me," she said jokingly. "I knew it was you. What's up?"

"I'm about to offer you entry into the wonderful world of in the field private detecting."

"Really. And what type of exciting and rewarding work do you have for me to do?"

"I'm glad you asked me that question. All you have to do is attend a fund raising dinner for James Cody. Andrea Newsome will be there. You just have to observe her actions and maybe take a few pictures if you see her doing anything interesting."

"Is that all? How will I be able to get into this dinner? Are you going to buy me a ticket?"

"Ticket. You don't need no stinking ticket. All you need is your handy dandy P.I. phony press pass. I'll drop them off to you. If you decide to undertake the assignment. This tape will self-destruct in ten seconds. So what do you say?"

"I say my boss wouldn't like it if he knew I was doing it. I think he's starting to have a major thing for Andrea."

"I won't tell him if you don't."

"He could come with her. What would I say to him?"

"I don't think he'll show for the fundraiser. I think they're in the 'let's dance, let's eat, let's screw like crazy' stage."

"Maybe that's so. But why should I do it? What are you offering me?"

"What do you want? I'll give you anything. A toaster, a twelve-inch black and white TV. A boom box. You name it, you got it."

"I want to go fishing in Michigan."

"Michigan? Fishing?"

"What's the matter? Don't you like fishing?"

"I like my fish cooked and on a plate. It takes too long to bag 'em out of the water."

"Then you won't go."

"I will go. If you do the job."

"I'll do the job."

The fund-raising dinner for Cody was being held in a good-sized hotel meeting hall. It had enough four, six, and eight-seat tables to handle a crowd of five hundred plus. To the left and right there was a portable bar set up. Waiters and waitresses also milled about toting trays of drinks. Out in front of a raised podium were four long tables filled with five or six types of meat, vegetables and pastries.

The crowd consisted of the staple of Republican support. Rich or semi-rich white businessmen, their wives, daughters, and friends, with a sprinkling of up and coming yuppies and minority group members.

Michelle moved down the hall toward where the fundraising dinner was being held. She was dressed in a white collarless blouse, black suit coat, and black slacks. She was carrying a purse with a shoulder strap.

Michelle reached the entrance. It was being manned by a geeky looking guy in a tux.

"Good afternoon, miss. Do you have an invitation?"

Michelle took a wallet from her coat pocket and flashed it at the geek. "Print journalist."

"For what publication? Let me see that ID again. Ebony magazine." The geek checked the pad he pulled from his pocket. Ebony. Ebony. Ebony. I don't see it on my list. I'm sorry."

"Okay. But you see, I'm not really with the magazine now. I quit to write a book. But I'm a stringer for The Defender. I don't have a card yet."

He checked his list again. No Defender either."

"I don't know. It must've been an oversight. But I'm sure Mr. Cody wants to get his story out to the black community. At least that's what he said on television last week."

"All right, all right. I guess it's okay for you to go in."

"Thank you."

Michelle stepped into the hall. To her, the place smelled of money, power, food, and the kind of overpriced perfume rich women loved to buy.

She began to move along the outer edges attempting to pick Andrea out of the crowd. Michelle spotted her in a group of five people, Cody included. They were talking and drinking together. Five minutes passed. The aroma of the food was enough to lure Michelle to the buffet layout. She was impressed that there were real plates available instead of those paper ones that easily sagged. A tiered tray of cheesecake seemed to be calling her name. She lifted a slice. One bite was enough to win her over.

She had to give it to the Republicans. They really knew how to dish out the eats.

She was in the middle of eating her second piece of cake when she glanced over and saw Andrea leave the pack and start across the room. She stopped and sat at a table with the deep-tanned white-haired man she met with at a restaurant previously.

Michelle's interest peaked when the pair appeared to be engaged in an intense conversation. It popped into her head that she had the mini camera Ellis had given her. She unzipped her purse, dug around and came up with a the palm-sized camera. She casually moved over and sat at an empty table that gave her a good angle on Andrea. Between munching on her cheesecake, she placed the hand that held the mini camera on the table top. She periodically snapped photos of Andrea and the man.

Michelle left the table and went into a mingle mode. There wasn't a rush by those present to converse with her. She received some questioning looks, probably because she couldn't be placed as one of the few minorities that frequented their world.

She scanned the room looking for the right type of person. Her eyes landed on a woman in her fifties, who wore an expensive basic black dress, and looked like an aging perky cheerleader.

Michelle took a pad and pencil from her purse as she approached the woman. "Excuse me. How are you? I'm with The Chicago Defender. May I speak with you a moment?"

"Well, yes, I suppose you can."

"I'm assuming you're a supporter of Mr. Cody, and a loyal Republican."

"Yes, I am."

"As a woman, I've always been curious as to why you support a Party that sometimes takes positions contrary to the best interests of women."

"Well, I don't know that I agree with that. The Party is good for my husband's business, so it's good for me. That's not such a bad thing, is it?" The woman flashed a broad smile.

"I suppose not. I want to ask you something else. The lady over there in the purple dress. Somebody told me she was a political consultant. Do you know her? Is it true?"

"Oh, yes. That's Andrea Newsome. She handles James' campaign."

"I may want to interview her. Is the man with her a co-worker?"

"Oh no. That's Alfonso Vega. He's an international businessman and commodities broker."

"Really. Very interesting."

Michelle insisted on having breakfast with Ellis at the same diner as before. She had just informed him of the happenings at the fund-raising dinner. She dug into her purse and came up with the mini camera. She slid it across the table to Ellis.

"Here you go. I don't know how they came out. I'm not a photographer."

"But you play one at fund-raisers. Thanks. Uh, I may need you to do a run-down on this Vega guy."

"I knew you would ask that. It's going to cost you another three hours on the fishing trip."

"Cool. I'm hoping this guy might be the key to something. I need something that'll bust the case open."

"You'll get it," Michelle said, smiling. "I have a lot of confidence in your ability."

Chapter 21

On her lunch hour, Michelle was busy digging into the background of Alphonso Vega. It was much easier these days with the advent of the information super highway. If direct information wasn't available there were software programs and access to database material. In some cases, she was able to get a listing of newspaper and magazine stories about Vega. Getting accurate information concerning his business holdings and practices could be more difficult. Calling in favors from contacts in the business and law enforcement worlds might be necessary. She was determined to get the job done. She wasn't sure why pleasing Ellis was becoming more and more important to her.

Ellis was in his kitchen mopping the floor. He had just finished washing a sink full of dirty smelly dishes he hadn't bothered to get to previously. What he needed was a maid or wife. Considering the attitude of most women, a maid would be the best bet at getting the cleaning done.

The phone sounded off. Ellis put the mop down and hurried into the living room. He lifted the receiver.

"Hello."

"Are you Ellis Mason?"

"Yeah."

"Ain't you been trying to git Armad Drew off for killing Donna Beck?" a young black woman asked.

"That's right."

"I know something that can help get Armad off."

"Yeah, what is it you know?"

"I can't talk about it on the phone. You can come to my crib, and I'll lay it on you."

"The last time I did that I took an unwanted dive down a flight of stairs."

"Oh, I'm sorry to hear that. But I'm being for real. I swear."

"Will you meet me in a public place, like a restaurant or even a library?"

"No. No. Somebody might see me. You know how crazy peoples is these days."

"What about a movie theater. We can meet in the dark."

"No. No. People might see me on the street. You have to come to my crib. That's just the way it's got to be. I'll give you the address. Come in an hour or so. After dark."

Ellis took the 'fool me once, but don't fool me twice' attitude toward the proposed meeting. Before changing into a black T-shirt, black jeans, and a light navy blue jacket that came down below his waist, he retrieved his registered .38 Smith and Wesson and placed it in a belt holster. He also had a four-inch derringer he obtained from an electronic gadget salesman as a throw-in. He fitted the derringer's holster in the middle of his back, ala Peter Gunn from the old television series.

Ellis figured it was a fifty-fifty chance he was being set up again. He thought about bringing in an operative to help, but decided against it. If it was a set-up, they might back off if he brought someone else with him. He would rather just put himself at risk and let things play out to whatever conclusion.

Night had fallen when Ellis arrived at the address the woman who called herself Cynthia had given him. It was an L-shaped ancient looking brownstone located on a corner. There was a street and avenue entrance to the three-story building.

Ellis left the parked car. He chose the front entrance due to the apartment number he had been given. He would either be right or have to journey to the other end of the building.

Inside, he climbed the stairs to the third floor. The hall was dimly lit and not too sweet smelling. He turned to the right and found he had been correct regarding the 302 apartment number.

Ellis unzipped his jacket. He wanted easy access to his weapon, but he didn't want to scare the woman if she was a legitimate lead. He knocked on the door and smiled.

A slight-framed black boy of twelve cracked the door open. "You that Ellis Mason man?"

"Yeah. Where's Cynthia?"

"She's up on the roof. She said for you to meet her up there."

"The roof. Why there?"

"I don't know. She just said to meet you there." He pointed to a door at the near end of the hall. "That's the door down there."

"Okay. Thanks."

Ellis moved to a door with a faded sign that said: stairs. He opened the door. The bulb offered just enough light to see the individual stairs. He climbed the creaking stairs. The second door opened to the inside. He slowly turned the knob until he heard a click. In a quick jerking motion, he yanked the door toward him. The move was followed by silence. He took two steps down and then went to the top of the stairs.

Ellis saw no one when he stepped out onto the roof.

"Cynthia! Cynthia! Are you here?"

"I'm over here," said the voice Ellis had heard on the phone.

Slowly, Ellis moved around the corner of the roof. On that side there was a four foot high box-like enclosure that housed the building's electrical system.

"Where are you?"

"I'm behind the box."

Relaxing, Ellis moved within six feet of the box. He was stunned into red alert when Pike emerged from behind the box, armed with a 9mm handgun. He instinctively made a move toward his gun holster.

"Don't try it," Pike warned. "You'll be too late. Take the gun out with two fingers and slide it over here. Don't make me ask you again."

Ellis removed the .38 with two fingers and slid it ahead of him. It landed near the box.

"Why did you bring me here with your voice act?" Ellis asked.

"We tried to warn you before. But you wouldn't git off it."

"Then it was you, Mr. President. Or should I say Mr. Pike?" Ellis glared right into his eyes. "You shot J.C, didn't you?"

"If you talking about that little black bastard that got in my way, yeah, I took his ass out."

"You did Donna Beck and Francine Darden."

"Don't know 'em. Never met 'em. Congratulations. You've given me a good goddamn reason to whack your ass."

"You don't have to do it. I have no proof."

"But you wouldn't fucking stop until you got it. But I'm gonna be nice. I can pop you right now or you can run and dive off the edge. It'll be a terrible accident. Hell, you might even survive the fall."

"Screw you, man. I'm not dancing to your tune. Go ahead and shoot!"

"Cool."

Pike pointed the 9mm at Ellis' head.

"Wait a minute. Don't shoot. Don't shoot," Ellis begged, waving his outstretched arms in front of himself. "I'll jump. I'll jump."

"Do it, chicken ass."

Pike took aim and stepped forward.

Ellis backed up rapidly. He flopped to the roof on his buns. He scooted backwards by kicking his legs. He held up his left hand.

"Don't shoot. Please. I'll jump. I'll jump," Ellis said fearfully.

Pike laughed. "You really are a chicken ass."

Then Pike did what Ellis wanted him to. He lowered his gun. While sliding backwards, Ellis reached behind him and drew the derringer. In one motion he aimed and fired. A perfectly placed bullet caught Pike directly between the eyes. He seemed stunned that he had been hit. He grunted gutturally and moved like he wanted to mount a charge. Two steps into it he flopped flat on his face and remained motionless. His gun slid a short distance from his outstretched arm.

Ellis rose to his feet. He went to where Pike lay and gripped his wrist, searching for a pulse. None was present. It had come to that. He had killed a man. On the heels of Pike's revelation, he expected to feel some sense of relief. All that was there was an empty feeling in the pit of his stomach.

After several seconds had passed, he snapped back into action. He removed a handkerchief from his pocket and wrapped the derringer in it. The derringer was placed in his jacket pocket.

No one was in the hall when Ellis descended the stairs. He went all the way down to his car and got on the cellular phone. He dialed the police and made a 'shots fired' report. He then called Boulware at home and told him about the shooting. He urged him to beat the homicide crew to the scene, and maybe be there to run interference for him.

Ellis paced about in the hall until a pair of uniformed cops showed up. A stocky Hispanic and an almost too thin black guy.

"Do you know anything about the shots fired report?"

"Yeah. I made it." Ellis handed the cop his private investigator ID. "I'm a private detective. A guy on the roof drew on me. I shot him with this."

He took his ID back and handed the gun in the handkerchief to the cop. The cop unwrapped it.

"A one-shot derringer. You were cutting it close."

"It had to be that way."

"Let's check the roof."

"Wait. One of us has to stay here. In 302, a kid sent me up on the roof. He might know something abut the man I shot."

"I'll stay," the Hispanic officer said.

Ellis and the black cop went up the stairs to the roof. They moved directly to the body. The cop pulled out a flashlight and snapped on the beam. He kneeled and examined the body.

"He's gone. Why didn't you call it in as a shooting death?"

"I didn't know he was dead when I made the call."

"How did this happen?" the cop asked as he rose to his feet.

"I was expecting a woman when I came up here. Instead, this guy popped up from behind the box and drew on me. He made me throw my gun over there by the box. Then he wanted me to jump over the edge. I went with it, and then pretended to fall. That's when I drew and shot. I guess I was pretty damn lucky."

"You did some nice thinking under fire. Do you know the man? Have you seen him before?"

"No."

"Well, let's check out the kid."

Ellis and the cop returned to the hall. Ellis continued on to where the Hispanic cop was standing near apartment 302.

"I guess we can check on the kid."

"Okay, amigo."

The cop banged on the door hard. After a few seconds, the boy cracked the door open. When he saw the officer there he tried to slam it shut, but the cop stuck his foot in the door and banged his shoulder into it hard enough to overpower the kid and make his way inside.

The room was devoid of furnishings except for a ratty looking sofa and a folding chair.

The boy was about to take off running until he saw Ellis come in behind the cop.

"Hey, I'm back. Surprised to see me?"

"I don't know. I was expecting the big man. He still owes me a ten spot."

"For doing what?"

"Just to tell you to go up on the roof to find some woman named Cynthia."

"Do you know the big guy's name?" the cop asked.

"Naw. He didn't say. I didn't ask him. I just wanted the thirty dollars."

"Come on, Chico, you could've been facing an accessory charge. I could still haul your ass to juvenile hall. Tell the truth. Do you know the man's name?"

"Naw. I swear. I was just hanging. He called me over and asked me if I wanted to make some quick money. I swear. That's all it was. Can I go now?"

"Go. And watch who you take money from."

Ellis was seated on the bottom step of the stairs. The Hispanic cop leaned against the doorsill. Boulware reached the top of the stairs, looked around, and approached the pair of men.

"I'm Sergeant Boulware. Homicide."

"You got here fast," the cop said. "We have a shooting up on the roof. It looks like it might be justifiable. This is Mr...."

"I know who he is. What have you done this time, Ellis?"

"I survived a life threatening situation."

"Let's go up and see what we've got."

Ellis and Boulware stepped out on the roof. The black officer was stationed near the body. They walked over to him.

"What's up, Sarge?"

"I'm cool. You better go down and show the crew the way up when they get here. You know they won't know their ass from a hole in the ground."

"Yeah. Okay."

The cop moved on and left the roof.

"Okay. What's the story?"

Ellis gave him the story from the phone call to the shooting.

"Do you know who the hell this guy is?"

"Yeah. Mongo Pike. He's a small-time hit man, among other things. At least, he was. Man. He admitted to shooting J.C."

"Can you believe him?"

"He had the drop on me. So he had no reason to snow me. I don't know how we can confirm it, though."

"What did he say about the two women?"

"Nothing. He claimed not to know them."

"Maybe we could tie the weapon that killed Miss Darden to him. Or maybe we could uncover a connection between him and Sammy Hendrics. But first things first."

Boulware took a pair of tight fitting leather gloves from his coat pocket. He slipped them on. He kneeled and pulled a wallet from one of Pike's pockets. He searched through the plastic card holders.

"I have an ID card with an address. I hope it's current."

Boulware slid the card out of the plastic and stuck it in his pocket. He returned with the wallet. He checked the opposite pocket and came out with a ring of keys. Two appeared to be to a vehicle. Three more looked like house keys. He removed two of the house keys from the ring. The rest were returned to Pike's pocket.

"We can possibly get the jump on the crowd tomorrow," Boulware said, coming to his feet.

"You must be really seeing things my way."

"A little bit. But don't get carried away with yourself." Boulware drifted away from the body. "We picked up something very interesting about Miss Darden that ties into your theory. We found a key to a safe deposit box. Inside the box she had several bank books from local branches. They all had a pattern with their deposits. For about ten months she made a steady stream of deposits from between two and five thousand dollars. That's above her salary by a long shot. How do you figure it?"

"Part-time drug dealer. Great investments."

"Or a little help from a friend. For the last five months she's been banking an additional eight to ten thousand."

"Another friend."

"Or maybe blackmail. People have been murdered behind stuff like that."

"I hear you."

"You ready to tell me what you're still holding back on?"

Ellis smiled. "I'm not holding back. Except for the political thing that doesn't seem to matter now."

"I hope you're being straight with me. For both our sake's. Did you tell them you knew Pike?"

"No."

"Then we'll probably be able to take our shot in the morning."

Chapter 22

Ellis was in bed asleep. It was a restless sleep. He constantly tossed and turned, flailing his arms about. He popped awake feeling hot and sweaty and out of sorts. Sighing, he forced himself to stretch and lean against the headboard. He wanted a drink of water. He wanted to take a leak, but he wasn't able to budge.

His mind went to the case and its strange mix of characters and motivations. Putting two and two together and coming up with four was easy enough, but how about working the right twenty and twenty and coming up with the right combination of forty.

A wave of tiredness swept over Ellis, almost as if he hadn't slept at all. He flopped back down on the mattress. His mind raced over images of the players in the case. Armad trying to convince him that he didn't kill Donna Beck. Royce wondering what he was up to on the night they met in the street. The down-beat statement on Francine's face before she walked out of the bar and was gunned down. The body language that went on between Royce and Andrea when they met at her apartment. The upbeat mood J.C. was in when they double dated. And Michelle, sweet Michelle. Someone he wanted to know better.

Ellis was hoping for a counting sheep effect. Whether it worked or not, he did drift off to sleep. A short time later, the ringing phone jolted him awake. He reached over to the night-stand and lifted the receiver.

"Hello. You have me."

"Ili. Are you up yet?" Boulware asked.

"Not quite."

"You better hop to it. I'm running your way and then we can go on to Pike's."

"I'll be ready."

Ellis was set to move when Boulware arrived. He entered the car and they drove off together.

"So, how did you sleep last night?" Boulware asked.

"Pretty good."

"Like hell you did."

"Okay, you caught me," Ellis admitted.

"It's rough after you shoot somebody. Even if they were out to pop you."

"It happened to you?"

"Yeah. Twice. One of the guys died. It'll be rough for awhile, but you'll get over it."

"I guess."

Pike's house was located in a far south side neighborhood of single family homes. It was a compact ranch style place covered with lime green aluminum siding.

Ellis and Boulware left the car and approached the house.

Boulware used the key he got off the body to unlock the door. They stepped into a room cluttered with assorted junk. Dirty clothes, old newspapers, and empty beer cans were scattered everywhere. A half-eaten sandwich on a table had several roaches munching on it.

"He was a great housekeeper," Ellis quipped.

"We better check the bedroom first. That's where people usually stash stuff."

The bedroom was in about the same shape. There was a dresser along the wall, a queen size unmade bed, and barely enough space for a full length pool table. The walls were plastered with centerfold photographs from girlie magazines. Three boxes of magazines were jammed up against a wall.

They walked into the room.

"I guess he was into pool," Ellis said.

"Or pool table sex. I'll take the dresser."

Ellis moved to the boxes of magazines. He thumbed through the top ones in each box.

"Porno, motorcycle, and Marvel comics. A well-rounded reader."

"Damn. A mouse. Jesus."

"You lucky you didn't find a rattlesnake."

"I think I have something here."

Ellis turned and saw Boulware with a brown nine by twelve envelope. He moved over as Boulware pulled a clipping from a magazine article from the envelope.

"It's an article about a big time international business guy. Alfonso Vega."

"Why the hell would Pike be reading an article like that?"

"Don't know. Something in here might tell us."

Boulware dumped the contents of the envelope onto the dresser top. They sifted through the contents. Ellis lifted a hand written note. It said:

Dear Zeke,

Here's a couple bad-ass investments for us to make. We can cash in even more on our short-haired little babe. Try this out. Channel 25 stock. Two For One Videos.

Ellis read the note and then handed it to Boulware.

"I wonder who this Zeke guy is. Andrea Newsome. I think she has short hair. Channel 25. Channel 25. I remember reading that some big company was planning on buying the station and turning it into a super station like WGN. I wonder when the note was written. I guess it never got to this Zeke. But you know more about all this, don't you?"

"Man. Why do you keep saying that?" Ellis asked with a smile.

"Because it's true. I've been a cop long enough to read people. Even a poker face like you. I figure you think you can sort this out better than we can. Maybe you can. I'm gonna give you the rope to go ahead and do it. If you put a noose around your neck, don't expect me to save you from a hanging."

Ellis returned to his house with thoughts about the case swirling through his head. The more he paced about and thought, the more things jumbled together in his mind. He finally gave up. He sat near the end of the sofa and secured a pad and pencil from the telephone table. He decided to compile a list of players with known connections to each other.

1. Armad Drew, Donna Beck, Francine Darden

2. Francine, Walter Ryan, James Cody, Andrea Newsome

3. Donna Beck, Francine Darden, Mongo Pike, Zeke Wilson, Andrea

4. Francine, Andrea, Vega, Pike

Ellis kept looking at the list and running the events of the case through his brain. He began to see the case as a solar system. The three murders were the sun and the players, money, and motivations were the planets that revolved around it. To be king of the universe, all he had to do was arrange all the elements in the correct order.

Ellis paced about in a semi-circle for three minutes. He suddenly had all the planets in place. All he had to do was close the thing down. His problem was he knew he couldn't close it alone.

"Goddamn you! You son-of-a-bitch. Why couldn't you just let it be?" Royce came from behind his desk and began to pace about. Ellis was standing nearby. "Why couldn't you just let it be?"

"How could I?"

"Why couldn't you? That guy you shot admitted to killing your partner. Can't you be satisfied with that?"

"You know I can't. If one of your operatives was murdered, you wouldn't stop until you got everybody that was responsible."

"Bullshit! I don't wanna hear it."

"Come on, man. You have to hear it. I can't just let this slide. I mean, it's not just some little white collar scheme. People were murdered."

"I don't care about that crap. You're trying to cut me in half here."

Ellis backed off, afraid he might lose Royce completely. The silence in the room was deafening. Ellis moved in closer.

"Look. I know you have a personal stake in all this. But you just have to look beyond it and try to see what I'm going for here."

"Why are you bringing this to me? Why don't you take it to the goddamned police?"

"It's a tough sell to the cops. They have Armad for Donna Beck. And Hendrics for Francine. And J.C. Hell, they think it was a random shooting. They probably don't expect to solve it at all. I need to present the whole package to them and drop it in their laps. I can't. I can't do it without you."

Sighing, Royce drifted over to the window. He ran both hands backwards through his hair. "The next time I bring up any Bogart stuff, somebody please kick me in the head." He turned and faced Ellis. "Okay, I'm in."

Chapter 23

I t was later in the day. Ellis and Royce were still together in Royce's office. The tension in the air was way down. Ellis had turned a radio to an FM jazz station, hoping to create a soothing, low key mood. Royce had sent a secretary to his apartment to retrieve a light blue summer suit. At this time, he was dressed in the suit pants, white dress shirt, and a red and blue striped tie. The suit coat rested on the sofa in the office. Ellis was seated a couple of feet from him. He had changed into a cotton shirt with a wide and deep pocket on the left side. A pair of work coveralls were on the sofa next to him.

Royce had already called and made a date with Andrea. Lately, she had been attempting to cook for him. Most of the meals were decent, at best. However, she did hit her stride when it came to preparing steak and potatoes and onions. Royce had requested that she prepare her specialty for him.

Ellis checked his watch. "I guess we better start moving on this little operation."

"Yeah."

They went to the desk. A topless box was present. From it Royce removed a tie clip that doubled as an electronic listening device. He slipped the device onto his shirt and tie. Ellis lifted the bug's monitor from the box. It was the size of a Walkman and even had an earphone attachment. He placed the monitor in his shirt pocket. The earphone cord was wrapped around his neck. He got into the coveralls and zipped them, leaving enough cord exposed to reach his ear. Royce put on his suit coat without buttoning it.

"Don't forget the walkie-talkie," Royce said.

They each took walkie-talkies from the box before exiting the office.

Ellis and Royce rode to the ground floor in an elevator.

"Uh, I want to thank you for helping me out on this. I don't know if I would do it if I was in your position."

"You would."

They reached the parking lot. Royce went to his Mustang. Ellis moved to his car. From the glove compartment he took a .32 Colt automatic. With the safety on he placed the .32 in the deep pocket of the coveralls.

Ellis crossed the lot to a van with the same markings and colors as the electric company. Inside, he watched Royce's car pull out of the lot and hit the streets. He gave the Mustang a three-minute head start before activating the walkie-talkie.

"Hey, have you got me?"

"Ten-four, good buddy, and all that stuff."

"I'm ready to test our little gadget. Give me a few seconds and then start talking."

Ellis snapped on the monitor-recorder and put the earphone in place. Through it he heard Royce say, "You're going to owe me big time after this, you know. If I need you to work a case, you better say yes."

Ellis spoke into the walkie-talkie. "I hear you. I will say, yes, yes, yes. I'll pay it back to make sure I have it on tape. If I don't get back to you, it's cool."

"Okay."

By the time Ellis reached Andrea's street in the van, Royce had already parked and entered the building. The plan was for him to use the janitor at work guise again. He would go to Andrea's floor and set up for a fake repair job while listening to the bug monitor.

Andrea, dressed in a simple sleeveless canary yellow mini-dress, crossed the room and opened the door for Royce.

"Hi, handsome."

"Hello, long, tall and sexy."

Andrea hit Royce on the lips with a smacking kiss. "Come on in. how do you feel?"

Royce stepped in and closed the door behind him. "You tell me first."

"I feel great. Like eating, drinking, and screwing your brains out."

"I'm not feeling too good myself. You shouldn't be. You recently lost someone that played a major role in your life these last few months."

Andrea sat in an easy chair and crossed her legs. "I don't know what you mean. Who are you talking about?"

"Francine Darden."

"Ryan's mistress? I told you, I never met the poor child."

"I know you did. I just don't believe you."

"Brad, what is this? I thought you were here for a meal. I feel like such a fool. I went through all the trouble of cooking. Instead, it's obvious you're here to grill me."

Royce moved over and sat on the sofa. "I'm not here to grill you. I'm here to clear my head. And to tell you a story. It's about two women that worked at the same brokerage firm. Both of them have recently been murdered. I believe they uncovered an insider's trading scam. A company called WCN, owned by an international mogul, Alfonso Vega, had plans of buying a local television station here in town to turn it into a super station. They also wanted to buy a regional video store chain and take it national. A broker with inside information could encourage associates to buy up as much stock as they could in the companies, and then watch the price soar when the sale is announced. There would be big money in it for all concerned. The women's big mistake was trying to blackmail those involved in the scheme. It reached a point where those involved were willing to kill to put an end to the blackmail."

Royce paused, as if he had to convince himself to continue. "The first woman killed was a black woman named Donna Beck. She would be just another inner city statistic. She even had an ex-con boyfriend who became a major suspect. Once his prints were found on the murder weapon he was charged in the case. These weren't stupid killers. They researched their targets. They found an ex-con school friend and paid him to smile in her face, and then pound her to death. This guy had a hit man friend that was sent out to eliminate the second woman. That's when this whole scenario starts to unravel. The hit man picked up on a second man that was tailing the woman also. Instead of backing off, he decided to take down the man that was blocking his way. But a disturbance happened at the motel location and he had to back off. He came back later and hit his target. That's just about the gist of the situation."

Andrea sat in silence with her mouth gaped open. "I cannot believe what I'm hearing. At least you didn't call me by name." She left the chair and stood directly in front of Royce. "How can you think this about me? Do you really think I'm some kind of sleaze factor, money grubbing witch that'll do anything to get what she wants?"

Royce rose to his feet with a look of unwanted anguish on his face. He gripped Andrea's shoulders tightly with his hands.

"You know I don't want to believe it. You don't know what it took for me to come here like this. Just... just tell me none of this is true. That you weren't involved. Convince me. Convince me and I'll do the same with Ellis and anybody else."

Andrea laughed in a quick, almost mocking manner. She left the arms of Royce and slinked across the room to a portable bar in the corner.

"You men are so amusing."

She lifted a glass and a bottle of gin. She poured herself a drink and gulped down half of it.

"Your scenario is pretty close to the truth. I had a relationship with an executive in the brokerage firm. When I heard about Vega's plan, I saw the possibility of making a big time killing. Because he's the type of man that always follows through on his plans. I put together a perfect network of dummy corporations and private investors. And that... that moron exec got careless and left a disk in his office computer. Those two bitches got hold of it and began blackmailing us. There, you have it. My little confession. Now, come over here... Come on."

Royce left the sofa and moved closer to the bar. "What?"

"I'm making you an offer. Thirty percent of what we make from the deal. The amount you can make will be staggering. I'm sure your black detective friend doesn't have any concrete proof. Make him believe he doesn't have a case, or eliminate him. Either one could mean big money for you."

"Andrea, I just don't understand this. Why did you have to do it? You have a great job making great money. Why do you need to make so much more?"

"Darling, it's the American way," she said, finishing off her drink. "You make all you can when you can. I want the good life. And I don't want to work forty years and retire to some cramped condo in Florida. You can do the same thing."

"I'm sorry. I can't."

"Too bad. But I thought you might say that."

Andrea walked around to the other side of the bar. From under the shelf she drew a .25 caliber pearl-handled automatic.

"Come on. Put the gun away. You're not serious."

"Oh, but I am," Andrea said with conviction.

"How will you explain the gunshot?"

"Darling, I always have a plan."

Keeping her aim and her eye on Royce, she backed around to the television. She snapped on the set. The VCR was activated. On the screen a movie shoot-out was taking place.

At that moment, the door flew open, Ellis having kicked it in. Andrea turned to face him. He raised his gun and fired first. She was hit in the shoulder. Her gun went sailing from her grasp as she stumbled backwards and landed on the sofa. Royce dove over the back of the sofa, rolled to his feet, and scooped up the loose gun.

Ellis approached Andrea and glared at her. "I knew I was right about you."

"Go fuck yourself, you son-of-a-bitch. You've destroyed me and Brad, you cold-hearted bastard!"

Ellis' smile came slow and easy. "It takes one to know one."

Epilogue

It was a sweltering summer day in Chicago. The combination of heat and humidity had driven thousands of people to area beaches. The one along Lake Shore Drive was no exception.

Royce sat under a tree in a grassy spot several yards from the beach. He was wearing light gold pants with a matching collarless shirt.

Ellis came on the scene wearing three-quarter length short pants and a tank top. "Hey, how you doing?"

"I'm doing a little better. How about you?"

"Same here." Ellis sat down next to Royce. "I'm not having the dream where I shoot Pike on the roof and he breaks into a hundred pieces. And then the pieces grow out into clones of Pike. They all chase me and I jump off the edge of the building. I won't miss having that one."

"I'm still having the one where I'm set to marry Andrea. Only I can't find the church where the wedding is supposed to take place. So I'm driving around frantically going from church to church. I always wake up before I find the right church... So much for that crap. What's the latest on the case?"

"I checked with the state attorney's office yesterday. They're still gathering information for indictments or for a grand jury. Andrea and the rest are under orders not to leave town. They're still looking for Zeke Wilson and a guy named Benny Carr, who might've been in on the blackmail scheme with Donna and Francine. Do you think Andrea will skip when push comes to shove?"

"Who knows? Who, who, who?"

Ellis chuckled. "You sound like an owl with all the whoing."

"I probably feel like one too."

"I threw caution to the wind and upgraded my computer system. I suppose it'll be worth it if I get a few more satisfied customers."

"There you go. If you don't watch out, you'll become a good businessman in spite of yourself."

"You know me. Always thinking. Always thinking."

www.ingramcontent.com/pod-product-compliance
Lightning Source LLC
Chambersburg PA
CBHW052135170626
46812CB00004B/1437